When I Was Young and In My Prime

When I Was Young & In My Prime

Alayna Munce

NIGHTWOOD EDITIONS
ROBERTS CREEK, BC
2005

The characters in this book are the product of fancy; any resemblance, in whole or in part, to any person, living or dead, is unintentional.

Published by Nightwood Editions
R.R. #22, 3692 Beach Ave.
Roberts Creek, BC, Canada V0N 2W2
www.nightwoodeditions.com

Edited for the house by Kathy Sinclair
Cover design by Anna Comfort

Printed and bound in Canada

Nightwood Editions acknowledges financial support from the Government of Canada through the Canada Council for the Arts and the Book Publishing Industry Development Program (BPIDP), and from the Province of British Columbia through the British Columbia Arts Council, for its publishing activities.

LIBRARY AND ARCHIVES CANADA CATALOGUING IN PUBLICATION

Munce, Alayna, 1973-
    When I was young and in my prime / Alayna Munce.

ISBN 0-88971-209-3 / 978-0-88971-209-6

I. Title.

PS8626.U53W48 2005   C813'.6   C2005-903448-3

...which is to say
a truth in nostalgia:
if we steel ourselves against regret
we will not grow more graceful,
but less.

— Jan Zwicky

orbiting

☙

I lie in the dark listening to the creak of the clothesline outside, shirts catching punches of wind. A siren whines listlessly for an emergency somewhere. Pigeons flap against the eaves and settle again. James sleeps beside me, his breath letting itself in and out of his body as if it's always lived there and always will.

I lie there with a fat lip of a heart, watch his eyelids twitch in the moonlight.

Eventually I pull my knees up and slip out from under the quilt, its dark wool squares cut from old men's suits. My side of the bed is against the wall, so I have to climb—gingerly— over him.

Some nights I stay in the kitchen, put the kettle on for tea, turn on the radio and trawl through bands of static for a voice to keep me company. Other nights I go to my desk and sit by the window, waiting for the sun to rise and relieve the streetlights, writing a little.

In the middle of the city, this delicate effort: to reel a clear voice in from the cluttered night air.

∂

HEYANDwho'llgimme50forthewashboardhere
who'llgimme50andgo50andgo

longest day of the year today

the old bird feeder on the dresser beside Mary's reading glasses

it's all downhill from here, Peter said

the creak of line through pulley

aerial, they call it

furrow by furrow 'til you can see the whole of the crop

Watch that step folks, the last one's a lu-lu

4

❧

The end begins with a whole fall and winter of Mom going to the house every weekend—every weekend, a new project. Occasionally she bargains with my stepfather until he agrees to go with her. Sometimes I tag along.

One week she untangles all the jewellery, making piles on the bedspread: to be cleaned, appraised, kept, given away. Piles according to size, worth, style. Costume jewellery here, heirlooms there. She throws out some unmatched earrings, puts others aside to be re-set. She finds hinged boxes for the rings. The details crowd until I feel as if I'm surrounded by setting cement and have to excuse myself to take a nap on the couch.

The next week Mom goes through the closet washing all the clothes, making Grandma try them on. The skirts and slacks and cardigans that no longer fit, she packs into green garbage bags, replacing them gradually over the course of the winter with brightly coloured oversized track suits on sale at Eaton's, the Bay or Sears. I can't help thinking I'd rather be a childless baglady than someday find myself wearing a fuchsia track suit.

This week we're going through boxes of old papers: letters, exams, bills, clippings, lists. Grandma is smiling, amiable, reading old Christmas cards from her students. She spots me in the door frame and, beaming, says, "Here, you can take these home with you if you like."

Mom reaches for them with an overly bright, "Thank you!" and puts them in the box of things to be thrown away.

A few minutes later Grandma is crying, demanding she

be allowed to keep the name tag from the UCW conference. HELLO my name is: *Mary Friesen*. And though Mom must know it would be so much better, so much easier to just let her have the thing, something in her won't give.

The house is a brick bungalow, trim and squarish, squatting on Silver Street in a subdivision on the outskirts of town. They bought it when they sold the farm, chose it for the double lot (which meant lovely big garden) and in spite of the swimming pool (which meant nothing but nuisance). No one has yet mentioned selling, but it's becoming increasingly obvious that the current arrangement isn't sustainable. So, though we don't talk about it, we are, like good Protestants, preparing for it.

I volunteer to sort the books. *The Scrabble Dictionary*, three bibles, an etiquette guide, *Grimm's Fairytales*. In among all the *Encyclopaedia Britannica* volumes and *Reader's Digest* condensed classics, I find two small five-year diaries of Grandma's from the '60s and '70s. The usual kind: leather bound with a flimsy gold lock, four lines for each day, five years worth of January first on the first page, five years worth of January second on the next.

Kneeling on the musty grey rug by a shelf in the far corner of the basement, I hesitate, taking a moment to sound the absence of a sound mind from which to ask permission. It's for form's sake, I suppose, more than anything else; as if a hesitation before an act of invasion somehow softens or buffets it.

Last Christmas, while rooting through some photo albums, I found a notebook of Grandpa's, a kind of journal or ledger from his farmhand days out west. It was clear to me in that case: permission should be granted before it was read. When I asked, he consented with a shrug so nonchalant that I wondered at first if he'd really understood what I was asking. Or maybe it was a shrug of resignation—one more invasion, one more indignity in the gathering mob of indignities that seemed to comprise old age. In the end, though, I settled on the assumption that the notebook simply represented a self so far gone he no longer cared about that character's privacy.

In the basement, with Grandma's diaries in hand, I hesitate politely, then pick one of the locks with a bobby pin.

It's filled: all four lines for all five years on almost every page. I start reading somewhere in October:

> Peter got new tires for the car today. Irene brought me a blue clothes hanger, covered. Tonight I attended "Our Wedding Gowns Past and Present" at the Paris Presbyterian Church, with Marjorie McPherson and Hazel Pelton.

Then the same day the next year:

> Did the washing. Singer Sewing Machine repair man fixed bobbin. Ruth telephoned tonight. Spent an hour at the piano. Letter to the Editor regarding moving War Memorial. Rick and Bonnie's 3rd son born (harelip). Turned Furnace on.

I flip back, to September: *Started new school year today. Fresh coat of paint on school. 16 students in my class, five of them new...* and the first and last names of the five new students.

I keep reading, skipping around—list after list of tasks completed, meetings attended, occasions marked.

> Peter and I drove to the funeral home this afternoon. Ruby and Lorne were there. Peter and I ordered flowers. It was very

7

warm. I don't seem to stand the extreme heat very well. Ruby gave us peas, already shelled.

Surely, I keep thinking, surely she must break out of it once in a while. There must be a little anger or elation. Confusion. Maybe despair. I look up Mom's wedding day. She describes the weather and the menu and writes, *What a lovely day for Ruth.*

I flip to my birthdate and read the calmly recorded fact of her first grandchild: weight, length, name and exact time of birth. I start to laugh—it's so absurd—and that's when Mom appears behind me and asks what's funny.

I'm surprised at how angry she is. "Well," she says, "you'd no doubt go on and on about all your feelings but she only had four lines."

The next morning I wake and remember I have the day off. Today I am not a waitress. Bliss. I lie in bed for a while, and when I remember the diaries, I find myself thinking about the few spaces here and there without writing, the days she didn't write.

I keep thinking about those days.

જ

I find myself thinking more and more about my grandparents. I try to think of them one step removed, as names, say, on a charity mailing list: Peter and Mary Friesen. Ordinary as can be.

Wandering the aisles of the No Frills supermarket around the corner from our apartment, I think about their garden and preserves. Their secret recipe for gooseberry jam. Their plastic milk bags of frozen green beans. How they pickled everything from plum tomatoes to asparagus to carrots, the jars lined up on shelves in their basement, an inconceivably intimate grocery store. How, when I was a child, the jars were a lovely quirk particular to my grandparents: no one else I knew grew and preserved their own food; it seemed an elegant and ingenious enterprise. How it took me years to realize it was simply the remnants of a mode of survival, universal, obsolete.

I sit on the streetcar and listen to people talk into cellphones, keeping each other utterly up to date (*Hi yeah I'm on the streetcar yeah just passing, uh, Dufferin, I'll be there in five minutes*). I listen and think about the one time my grandfather left a message on my answering machine, his voice hesitant like a horse's front hoof in the air, saying he'd bought the cabbages for the sauerkraut. His voice signing off like in a letter, *Okay then. Goodbye. Love, Grandpa.*

I lie awake in bed next to James and wonder about their marriage. What was left unsaid between them? What was simply understood? I'm only now beginning to see that sometimes words can dilute things between people. How do you tell the difference between leaving something unsaid to keep it pulsing and whole, and leaving it unsaid to avoid its whiff of discomfort and change? Are there things they always meant to say? Things that will never be said, now that their decline is so thoroughly underway?

Don't get me wrong. I don't think about my grandparents constantly. Relatively speaking, I hardly think about them at all. I think about my new schedule at work, and I think about the new waitress who has a pierced lip and an open relationship and whose cheeks are always ruddy and flushed as if she's burning at maximum efficiency. I think about time. I list errands in my head. I think about an off-handed comment James made last week about the woman who plays bass in his friend Dave's band, how sexy she looks when she concentrates, and was it really off-handed, and should I just leave it or ask. I think about a poem I'm working on and wonder how many more layers of certainty I'll have to scrape off it before I get to something that shines.

I lie there like a leaky flue.

≈

Longest day of the year today. Peter and I watched the sun set from the porch swing, and I had a feeling of unevenness, like a fever or undone shoelaces or a job left unfinished. *It's all downhill from here*, Peter said, and I couldn't for the life of me remember whether that phrase is meant to be uplifting or melancholy.

All downhill from here is good if you're walking or bicycling or pushing a cart, I thought, but it's bad if you take it to mean up is good. As in *things are looking up*, or *he's moving up in the world* or *the politics of this country have really gone downhill in the last few years*.

You know the kinds of things people say.

I didn't bother asking him, though, figuring that in the end it's all the same no matter what we say about it.

~

Some of the times in the morning I wait outside the barn door. Wouldn't say it's my favourite time. Not like a Sunday dinner during the tobacco harvest with all the crew eating their fill and the pickers flirting with the girls from the curing house and the one from Quebec telling funny stories in his French accent. No, waiting just outside the barn door of a morning isn't like that at all. Not something a person would look forward to. No, it's a thing that just happens every once in a blue moon. When I'm not looking for it. In spring, mostly. Stepping out of the barn in the dark after milking and something makes me stop. I can see the kitchen light on inside the house and Mary moving around from stove to sink. But I don't go in to her. I know my tea will be ready, but I don't go. I stand there and look out into the tobacco fields and... wait. Wait and watch. Until the sun lifts itself up there and the daylight takes the light of my lantern. I wait until the mist lifts too, furrow by furrow, 'til you can see the whole of the crop. See across the width of the field entire. And maybe catch a glimpse of the brown mare in the distance, the one Ruthie loves so much. Whenever I catch sight of that horse on the hill I always think to myself, she's too damn perfect, that beast. And Mary always keeps the tea warm for me, and never asks me why I lingered.

ॐ

I remember the porch swing, the heavy quilt tucked neatly under our thighs, spanning our laps: Peter Friesen teaching his granddaughter to whistle. Mary Friesen inside, still brisk and competent, still completely aware of where the compost was kept, what the coffee grinder was for. We'd come in to her later for bitter cocoa. We'd come in rosy-cheeked, and Grandpa would say he'd been teaching me to whistle. That was how I knew I was supposed to have been learning.

On the porch swing I'd just swing my feet and lean against him, and he'd whistle and whistle, sometimes getting an answer from a bird. A girl leaning up against an old Mennonite man from the Ukraine. A retired tobacco farmer who metamorphosed into bird after bird and then back into farmer by whistling a song rather than a pattern of sounds. His own call. Farmer in the dell. Old MacDonald had a farm. Farmer Brown he had a dog and bingo was his name-o. His cheeks and lips mysterious in their small manoeuvres behind the whistle. My head against his hard-muscled arm, the quilt made of old wool suits heavy on our laps, my end tucked under my thigh, wrapped carefully around my feet, his end loose and not quite covering him.

He had five languages, six if you included whistling. Bits of them would come out now and then—flung, spat or sing-songy. A rhyme about a rabbit and a hunter to teach me the numbers: *raz, dva, tre, chiteria, piotch*, something, something, *poogilliotch*. And the curses: *Ay-ay-ay, Matoushka ri Nanka!* I imagined the languages in him like darkly coloured rivers. Wine-coloured, soil-coloured, the black of his bread, the blood of his borscht, the worn colour of his leather boots, the rust colour of the saw blade in the shed. Dark. Rich. Foreign. I imagined they were what kept his muscles so hard. It was the languages. It was the languages I leaned up against on bright winter mornings outside, the porch swing creaking. Though he spoke English without an accent, I always thought it was the whistling in which he was most fluent. Pure sound, unencumbered by meaning. Unadorned. Relieved.

❧

Months ago, when I was here learning to make sauerkraut, I went through the front closet. The days were getting colder, and I was hoping to find a new winter coat. I came across one I liked and tried it on, then went to the kitchen to show Grandpa.

"Hey, do you ever wear this coat anymore?"

He looked up from the crock he was wiping dry. "Nope," he said, and looked down again.

"Do you think I could have it?"

He turned from me toward the bushels of cabbages we were about to shred for sauerkraut. "What do you want it for?"

"To wear, Grandpa."

"Suit yourself," he said. I took that as a yes.

When it came time to go, I stowed the coat next to the crock of unripened sauerkraut in the back seat of the car (a sexy old 1966 robin's-egg-blue Valiant borrowed from a bartender at work, and admired begrudgingly by Grandpa when I arrived). I drove back to the city, my pleasure at the coat's perfect fit tainted a little by his gruffness.

It's been four months since. I've been back for several visits in the meantime with Mom, but today is the first time I've come back alone, and the first time I've worn the coat. In fact, I haven't worn it much all winter. But one day a few weeks ago, in a second-hand shop near the hardware store where I was buying paint, I found a long soft olive-green scarf to go with it. Since then, I've been wearing the coat like it was always mine. James has been out of town on tour (a last-minute gig opening for a singer/songwriter slightly more up-and-coming than he is), and I've repainted our whole apartment and worked a long string of late shifts, alternating between waiting tables and painting, writing a little, talking to practically no one except, *You want another pint? Need some change?* One day, walking to the streetcar, I realized the old coat was the only thing I was wearing that didn't have holes in it.

Grandpa grunted when I came in wearing it this afternoon. I paused, trying to interpret the sound. It could have been a grunt of greeting and recognition. Or it could have been mild disgust. Or something far less communicable than any of that.

Now, in curtain-filtered dusk light, he's telling me stories, a rare mode these days. I keep still and watch his lips as he speaks—the bluish purple bumps on them, just where the wet inner lip shows itself. They've always been there. What are they? Blood blisters? Something to do with blood.

We sit at the kitchen table in the half-dark, two cups of bitter coffee between us. He speaks slowly, and my mind wanders during the pauses—*What time does my shift start? Why can't my tongue resist this canker? Shit I forgot to feed the cat before I left*—each thought a kite lifting into another corner of the kitchen. I'm able to keep each line of thought taut, circling him, and still follow the slow line of his story. Sometimes he pauses so long I think he's stopped, and one or two of the kite lines go slack, drop to the countertop.

Grandma's lying down in the front room. Every once in a while she calls out, "Peter?" He closes his eyes and, after a second, calls back, "Put your head down Mary, you're napping."

A minute later his eyes are still closed. I'm beginning to wonder if he's fallen asleep when he opens them wide.

"Had it made the year before I married your grandmother. A month's salary. Picked out that brown-green material. Wool. Houndstooth, they call it. Had it made by the tailor. Dammit. What was that man's name. Pollack. Slowacki. Stan Slowacki. Yessir. I was the talk of the town. Peter Friesen, Alf and Evelyn Dowswell's new farmhand with a houndstooth coat and a feather in his hat."

"The coat is older than your marriage," I say, looking from the bumps on his lips into his eyes. My coffee's finished but he's barely taken a sip from his.

"They don't make things like they used to anymore," he says. And for a moment I hear the phrase the way it must have sounded the very first time it was said.

❧

July 28, 1930

Now by golly for another chapter: I have been in Winnipeg the reason was the supposed-to-be circus which took place on the 26th of July. It was quite interesting, but most of all I liked the exhibition of the wild animals who were put in one cage and one man amongst them. Baby! didn't he fix them though, and all he had was a whip and a revolver with blank shells in it and a chair which he used as a shield. With all those animals like lions and tigers, leopards, wild cats, bears & others, I would not have wanted to stay in there with a couple of loaded guns and that fellow had the nerve to be in there with only what I said and do with them what he liked except petting them. I am just looking ahead for the big day I will leave again for the money-eating city called Winnipeg. How things will hatch out then, I will put down here without a doubt. With a little patience strong will good hope etc. one might find life interesting enough to have it worthwhile living for.

The expenses I made on this trip:

My fare on the train and streetcar.	*$1.85*
An underwear for the summer.	*.65*
The tickets to the circus.	*1.60*
And the ice cream and drinks roughly	*.85*
The total of my loss.	*$4.35*

(The money I spent on the big baboon Johnny Schritt is .75 train fare home + .80 circus ticket + .10 dinner + .15 streetcar = $1.90. Be gosh she's going down like the grain in the grain exchange.)

≈

February 5, 1971

Ice storm, driveway like glass. Astronauts
Alan Shepard, Edgar Mitchell landed on
moon 9:45 am today. Stuart Roosa orbiting.
We carved with soap today at school.

a list of birds

ॐ

1 the domestic goose (*anser anser*)

When he is six years old, there are two wars: the Russian Revolution and his war with the goose.

The path from the house to the garden is blocked by a gander from his mother's flock. Several times now he's been turned back, his shoulders beaten by the gander's wings, his bare legs clamped by the gander's bill. Told how he must grab the neck—just so, at the back of the head—

he enters the barnyard. War has always been about territory.

The goose charges, neck outstretched, wings flapping, bill open, hissing. The boy reaches, fumbles, falls to his knees, finally grips feathered muscle. Unsure for a moment what part of the goose he holds, he opens his eyes and stands—is soon seen by his mother from the kitchen window tapping the gander's head in the dirt, lecturing it, dragging it forward until the thing follows in submission.

Releasing the gooseneck, he feels five years older and free from that day on to walk anywhere in the yard his heart desires, the goose
                    hissing like
            hunger from a
distance.

ॐ

2 the great grey owl (*strix nebulosa nebulosa*)

Now he is a boy on his way home from school, where they
teach in Russian and he may not speak his mother tongue.

He passes a row of silver spruce in a fenced-in farmyard—
unusual. If a man plants trees they are always fruit trees, who
doesn't need fruit trees more than silver spruce?

Rumours of ghosts clamber about this house; its shimmering
evergreens glow and moan when you pass at night.

His sisters asleep in a row above him, he lies awake nights in
his place at the foot of the bed, turning the mystery over in
his mind. Sucking it slowly. Making it last.

Finally one evening he climbs the fence to see for himself—
taking care not to rip his pants or there'll be hell to pay when
he gets home—

goose-pimpled   he approaches the first tree sees
  nothing   moves aside a branch and

        holy mother

                a grey and stately owl

swivels its head.   He follows its gaze
  to the next tree and there   is another and
                another and

another   each tree loaded
with great grey owls   dozens of them

all swivelling their heads,

    calm, real.

ॐ

3 the ruby-throated hummingbird (*archilochus colubris*)

When he is seventeen he works on a farm near Winnipeg as hired man for a James Henry Lytle (*hypocrite and as big a windblow as any of the Lytles are, but a good man all the same*).

One day he's in the barn grooming the horses.
He hears a humming.

Out of the corner of his eye

                  a flash then

there it is   still   *suspended like Christ himself*   then

darting to   fro
   up   down

                like some kind of crazy pendulum.

Insect? Moth? Bird? He hasn't any idea what to make of it, thinks that, for all he knows, it could be a fairy, come to him with a message.

Smudges in the air where the wings should be—*like someone took a thumb to a fresh charcoal drawing.*

He lights the lantern—the hum audible all the while—and when the thing comes into view again its back is green as new metal and the light has sprung its black throat into a deep red.

Nothing like it in the Old World, that much is for sure.

And though he is late for the evening meal, and though he comes to them lightened with awe, and though they laugh and hoot and slap their knees saying, *Oh that's a good one, a fairy caught in the barn and can't get out, oh that's a good one, that is,* he falls asleep content in this new country.

The hummingbird will always be his favourite.

(*Try whistling that sound—can't touch it.*)

~

4 the starling (*sturnus vulgaris vulgaris*)

Though even he did not quite know it, he decided to marry
her one Saturday afternoon while standing in front of the
diner. Counting his change with the sun in his eyes, he
spotted her coming out of the general store. A
starling swooped close,

                    and she was not startled.

ھ

5 the red-winged blackbird (*agelaius phoeniceus*)

After share-growing tobacco in southwestern Ontario for seven years, moving his family nearly every spring to a better deal, he's finally saved a down payment for his own farm: ninety-eight acres of mediocre land with thirty-two acres of tobacco rights, a debt-load he's been trying hard to fathom.

Spring's come early this year—late March rain. The farmyard is bottomless with mud. The truck, loaded up and ready to move for the last time, spins its wheels in the melted lane, burrowing deeper and deeper.

Some say red-winged blackbirds are the real harbingers of spring.

The males come a week or two early—before the females. Come to claim their territory. Come bearing a red so handsome, so bold, so brand-spanking new it must mean God approves of machines.

At the moment the first bird touches down on the naked maple beside the rented house, the neighbours gain purchase in the pushing, truck wheels engage solid ground, and he honks the horn:

kong-ka-ree!

Landowners.
Think of it.

ॐ

6 the house wren (*troglodytes aedon*)

One year the wrens nest in the mailbox. (That's the year the crop suffers from too much rain.)

Another year the wrens nest in an empty clay flowerpot by the shed. (That's the year the crop suffers from too little rain.)

This year they nest in the pocket of his canvas winter coat which Mary has left hanging too long on the clothesline because three times in a row
just

when it dried
the sky up
and rained again.

ॐ

7 the barn swallow (*hirundo rustica*)

The morning he puts the question to his son he is near fifty.
His son is thirteen. Swallows flash in and out of the barn
above them.

*If you want the farm it's yours. We can start this summer shifting the
load. If not, there's no point me sticking it out alone. I'm not getting
any younger and the work isn't getting any lighter and it's a good time
to sell. I'll finish the season and sell in the fall.*

Choice is yours.

> A fork-
> tailed bird cuts
> between them. An awkward
> silence.

*I don't know what it is I'm gonna be, but whatever it is it's not gonna
be a farmer.*

The boy pronounces each word as if he's practised for this
moment.

The swallows twitter from their mud nest in the timbers.

It's done then, he says, and turns his back to finish the season.

~

8 the chimney swift (*chaetura pelagica*)

It's early evening and he's up the ladder, looking down the
chimney to figure the obstruction, when a plume of swifts,
sudden and soot-coloured, breaks
                                                      into flight.

(*When that ladder tipped away from the house and I knew in my
bones I was going over
I tell you time
          stood still*)

His wrist bone snaps when he hits the ground, breaks
                                                      through skin.

Alone—Mary at choir practice, the kids grown and gone—
he puts the ladder away with one arm, pens a note in childish
left-handed writing, and walks to the hospital where he is a
nurse (*a male nurse*, he always says), works six shifts a week.

(*Good thing we sold that farm I guess, moved to town.*)

Neighbourhood kids trail him, his bright
bone a silent piping in the failing sun.

☙

9 the winter wren (*troglodytes troglodytes*)

On the porch swing he tries to teach me the wren's song. My lips ache and my whistle is vanishing into the thin winter air. I can do the chickadee, the robin, the goldfinch and the sparrow but

　　　　　wrensong is slippery and insistent, more fishtail than birdsong.

To have a grandfather is to be spellbound and unsettled, to be surrounded by languages you can't speak.

~

10 the scarlet tanager (*pirana olivacea*)

When my parents' marriage ends my mother moves us to
the outskirts of Brampton; our new house (along with forty-
five others exactly like ours) crouches on a small circular
suburban street called Tanager Square.

Peter Friesen comes to inspect, sees the high-fenced yard.

Postage stamp, he mutters, and spits, *not enough room to grow
a bloody thing. And it must of been a damn fool who named the
place—you sure won't be seeing any tanagers*
here.

☙

11 the blue jay (*cyanocitta cristata*)

Aunt Anne was Grandpa's favourite sister.

She hated blue jays because they were greedy at her feeder.

And that is all I know
about Aunt Anne.

did the question
disturb you

What is it Like to Have Alzheimer Disease?

(from *Alzheimer: A Canadian Family Resource Guide*)

Another way to find out more about Alzheimer is to try to imagine what it is like to have it. Obviously, you can't know exactly what it is like. However, the following scenarios should give you some insights into what your family member is going through, and how he or she feels. All of the examples in the list happen to people every day; they were chosen because they are everyday occurrences that are analogous to having Alzheimer Disease. They are not signs of the disease.

Think about the last time you lost your car in a parking lot. How did you feel—frightened, angry, bewildered, panicky? Did you feel as though you might never find it?

How frustrated did you feel the last time a vending machine didn't work? It wouldn't give you what you wanted and it wouldn't return your money and nothing you did (kicking, hitting, swearing) made any difference.

Have you ever left your house and later were unable to remember whether you turned the stove off? Did you go back to the house to check? Did you call a neighbour to see if everything was all right at the house? Did you do neither of those things, and then worry the whole time you were away? Did you then become obsessive for a while, so that every time you left the house you went back to make sure the stove was turned off?

How did you feel the last time you met someone you knew and couldn't remember the person's name? How did you feel when you wanted to make an introduction and could not because you forgot a name?

～

Pussy willows for sale in buckets outside the corner store where I buy my cigarettes: sure sign of spring. Not to mention the fact that James and I are having twice as much sex as we usually do. But I know it's officially, officially spring when my neighbours Connie and Bill emerge from hibernation.

James and I live in a spacious one-bedroom apartment on the second floor of a once-grand, now-verging-on-squalid old house in Parkdale, one of Toronto's more liminal neighbourhoods (rich meets poor, crazy meets sane, old meets new, wild meets tame—meetings so haphazard and insistent that sometimes the aspect shifts, and you'd be hard-pressed to say which is which). Connie and Bill live on the main floor of the house next door. All winter we don't see them, then one day they come out. After that, they're around for the next four months, smoking on their porch, radio tuned to the oldies station. Billy used to be with the Hell's Angels. He's quiet, doesn't do much else besides smoke and mumble the occasional greeting, one hand stroking his stubble. He's always looking off into the distance, as if someone stole his bike some time ago and he's been marooned here ever since. Connie, on the other hand, never stops moving.

She was the first Native woman to ever be a supervisor in the Children's Aid Society, but she quit all that years ago, fed up with the generalities of policy trumping the particularities of people every time. These days she's planting seeds she stole from the seed heads of flowers she admired in other gardens last year—or, like yesterday, she's waving me over to give me a box of twenty-four jars of sun-dried tomatoes packed in olive oil. Connie volunteers at the food bank. "We got a whole truckload," she said, "but no one in the lineup will have a thing to do with them and the soup kitchen volunteers can't be bothered figuring out how to fit the things into a meal." Last week it was a truckload of kiwis. I looked up a kiwi jam recipe for her on the internet. Once last summer, as I was on my way out of the house for my morning walk, she summoned me over for a serving of the chicken cacciatore she'd made at four that morning because she couldn't sleep.

When James and I moved in four springs ago, she called out from her porch and introduced herself, then got me to follow her inside so she could give me a slab of carrot cake. I watched her transfer it from her Pyrex pan onto a green Styrofoam tray, the kind they use to package snow peas in the grocery store. I took it home and shared it with James. The cake was exquisite, moist as anything, thick cream-cheese icing. On my way out later that day, I spotted her still on her porch and called over, saying it was the best carrot cake I'd ever had.

The next morning there was a knock at my door: Connie with the carrot cake recipe written out on a piece of cardboard from a pantyhose package. "It's from the *Sun*," she said. "There's a helluva lot of oil in it."

Then she eyed me as if she knew all my secrets and said, "Don't skimp."

ॐ

Spring means time for a garage sale.

Though we've been organizing for weeks, the basement is still filled chest-high with artefacts. Mary and Peter Friesen have saved everything that has ever come their way. Wooden chairs—with cracked seats and spindles missing—float stranded in corners, legs in the air. There are striped and polka-dotted hat boxes with hats inside that look like birthday cakes. Cream separators and butter forms. A stepladder. A skill-testing puzzle of coat hangers, which I utterly fail to solve.

Three large boxes full of plastic milk bags, all slit open at one end, cleaned, folded once and bundled in stacks of twenty, wrapped with twine like presents.

An old violin with a bowed fretboard and a black-lacquered cardboard case.

Crates of Christmas ornaments, grade-school test papers, sheet music. Stacks of moth-bally quilts and old board games—Chinese Checkers, Yahtzee, Parcheesi, Monopoly, Scrabble and Clue—the boxes crushed and most of the pieces missing.

A small black album displaying sepia photographs of a flood.

Rows of glass-topped mason jars, some with labels saying what they once contained, some still full. Apple butter, 1973: the year I was born. Pickled asparagus. Homemade eye ointment. Plum jam.

The garage sale doesn't even make a dent. Grandpa is gruffer than I've ever seen him, and Grandma is hoarding trinkets, throwing subtle tantrums, shaken to see the contents of her basement appearing on the front lawn, haphazard and shabby in the sunlight, spread out suddenly in public, strangers taking it away piece by piece. She's by turns generous and fierce: "Would you like these dear?" offering me a stack of old *Reader's Digests*, then refusing to give up a red plastic poinsettia, clutching it.

When Grandpa finds out that Mom has sold the bird bath right off the lawn, gruff becomes bewildered. "I didn't even know it was for sale," he says. He says it in the tone of someone who's slept in because of a time change and missed something important. He keeps on saying it, to anyone who will listen.

~

things that might survive a lifetime

1 the answer to the question, what do you do?

This almost always survives a man's lifetime.

> *my great-grandfather was a farmer*
> *mine was a steelworker*
> *mine a butcher*
> *mine a preacher*
>> *my great-uncle was a harness maker*
>> *mine a labour leader*
>> *mine a soldier*
>> *mine gambled a fortune away*

2 refusals

Sometimes refusals
survive a woman's life: oh it was a scandal when Aunty May
refused that widower's offer of marriage.
(I have some of her paintings,
hang them as reasons why.)

And I am told my namesake, Great-Grandma Helena,
refused to marry her murdered husband's brother
until his invalid mother died—
said she wouldn't be a slave to another man's burdens.
For eighteen years she refused.
Then, after the funeral, accepted.

And Aunt Olga refused
to roast a chicken if she didn't have anise seed.

3 odd details

Aunt Anne hated blue jays
because they were greedy at her feeder.

And that, as I said, is all I know
about Aunt Anne.

(Oh yes!
and that she lived in a place called Turkey Point.)

4 secrets

Not the content, perhaps, but the
silence, the wariness surrounding them (a pocket
of stale air in rock where a living thing
is preserved for a time after death
then dissolves, leaving fossil).

The way the whole family lifted
a leg to step over Arnica the dog lying
in the kitchen doorway long
after Arnica was dead and gone.

5 habits and tricks

Grandma would buy no ketchup but Heinz, no grape juice
but Welch's, said toothpaste gets out certain stains and only
bought Crest, said baking soda takes away fridge odour and
only bought Cow Brand.

The elements
of daily life, more basic now than air earth fire water.

Nothing but Ivory soap, nothing but 2%.

In the grocery store, my hand is drawn as if by tractor beam to her brands.

6 a violent death

Almost fair, isn't it? How if you die, as they say, in an untimely fashion, at least the memory is likely to survive?

We all know (though can scarcely imagine) how Grandpa's father died in 1919. He was the overseer of an estate in the Ukraine amidst war and revolution—the landowners long gone, the peasants hungry. He held a meeting, decided to start the threshing early and pay the peasants out in grain. Slept that night in a neighbouring village for safety.

Next morning, pregnant wife at his side, on his way to the first day of threshing, two young men stopped him, demanding the ox and cart. He gave it up, helping his wife down and then was
     shot
through the neck as an
afterthought
        on the road
  blood   leaving him
    neutral and
red.

7 a grand story or two

The morning after I met James, we went walking in a
snowstorm and he told me one of the only stories he knows
about his great-grandfather:

One winter morning he decided to paint cherubs on the
living room ceiling, one on either side of the light fixture.
When he stepped down to look at his work the little angels
weren't balanced, so he painted another beside the smaller
one,
                    which called for another on the other side,
which called for another on the other
                            and on and on he see-sawed
through the day until his wife came home that afternoon to
a ceiling teeming with cherubs.

And though I try in general to be wary of romance, that
day I was thinking who knows? That day I was thinking,
Someday (ridiculous!) *maybe someday I'll tell my children*
(absurd!) *maybe someday I'll tell my children that* (madness!)
*I fell for their father because the morning after we met, we went
walking in a snowstorm and he told me his lopsided story*   yes

  that day I was in love with how one thing leads to another.

＾

When Father was shot at the estate where he'd been the
overseer—and a good one at that—Mother, and mind you
she was eight months with child at the time, she found a
man willing to escort us back to our village. Dangerous
times in the Ukraine. No way in hell a woman could make
that journey alone with six children and another on the
way. The arrangement she fixed was he'd take us home
in the landowner's horse and covered wagon in exchange
for keeping the beast and rig when he'd got us there. The
men who'd shot Father had taken our ox and cart, and the
landowner was long gone so Mother always said, how she
figured it, it was only fair.

It was a two-day journey home, Mother and the man
up front, Father's body wrapped in Mother's finest linen
tablecloth just behind them, we children at the back,
hanging our legs over the edge. In between, all our earthly
goods. Anything that didn't fit in the wagon got left behind.
When we arrived, the village men nailed a few pine boards
together into a box, and we buried him in the orchard. They
cut slits up the back of his suit and made it known among
the neighbouring peasants. So his grave would be left
undisturbed.

We spent a few years back in the village after Father was
killed before we got the passage to Canada. The road into
the village came over the hill, and there was a fair view of the
communal orchard from the top of it. In summer I'd crouch
up there on the hill hours at a time and let my eyesight go
loose so the orchard was a green pool and Father inside.

That orchard was the pride and joy of the village. Took years to cultivate. We Mennonites—the settlers I mean, my forefathers—they planted it. First thing they did when they arrived. The Ukrainian peasants, they were jealous as Judas over that orchard but, as Father used to say, it didn't just appear from nowhere.

That orchard had every kind of fruit you could want. Apples, peaches, pears, apricots, cherries, plums. Especially plums. Always plums. Zwieback buns with stewed plums. Or pluma moos with cream. Or plum plauts hot from the oven. And of course we dried plums to make prunes. And a mulberry hedge all around the orchard with silkworm cocoons all over it like an old wedding veil. So much dried fruit from that orchard. Even now, the insides of my cheeks water just thinking of the place.

I can remember standing there at Father's graveside trying to figure how many plums I'd eaten from that orchard over the years. How many plums in a dish of pluma moos, how many dishes of pluma moos in a month, how many months less the ones we'd been away at the estate.

The day we buried my father was my ninth birthday, and no one had to tell me I was head of the family now.

క్

I've taken a second part-time job to help pay off my student loan: attendant at a nursing home in the neighbourhood. White Eagle Retirement Home. Saw a sign in the window. I help old people wash themselves two nights a week. I have to say it worries me slightly that my experience at a summer camp for disabled kids when I was sixteen seems to be good enough for them.

First shift last night. Ninety-seven-year-old woman, nearly deaf, pulls the call-bell. When I come in she's puking in her garbage can, vast amounts of diarrhea in her commode, both of which, I realize, will have to be dealt with by someone. The other worker, Barb, points me to where I can find disposable rubber gloves and goes off to call an ambulance. I manage, just barely, not to puke myself. When I'm done the woman pulls me toward her hearing aid and shouts into my ear, "Oh I feel bad." This somehow without self-pity; just information. Eventually the ambulance comes. Barb has the foresight to take out the woman's hearing aid and teeth so they don't get lost at the hospital. "Just in case she comes back," she says.

In between giving baths I do laundry. Folding pee-stained underwear fresh from the dryer. Such unearned intimacy, I could weep.

At the end of the shift Barb asks me what took so long when I showered Edith. I said we had a hard time getting the temperature right. The look she gives me over her glasses tells me quite clearly she thinks I'm too soft to last.

෨

I walk up to Queen Street wearing my new red leather satchel and my grandfather's well-cut wool coat. When I get to Queen and Lansdowne I suddenly feel self-conscious as I sometimes do at that corner among the sockless addicts and the latest wave of immigrants. I walk toward the greengrocer, downtown Parkdale, feeling stuck-up and well-to-do.

After the greengrocer I walk to the video store to return a video, thinking to myself, *I don't even have a VCR or TV, have to borrow them from my downstairs neighbours if I want to rent a video*; wanting, absurdly, to tell this to the men with the bottles sitting on the bench outside the store as I turn to go in; wanting, also, to tell them, *It was a big decision for me to buy this satchel*; knowing all the while I think this that no matter what I have or don't have, buy or don't buy, I'm rich and could say nothing to these men about it. I push the door to the video store open more forcefully than I need to, sick of myself.

When I come out of the store, a tall skinny guy stops me. He's younger than the men with the bottles, limp orange hair and freckles, tobacco stains the colour of old newspaper at the corners of his mouth. "Hey miss," he says, putting his hand out toward my arm but not quite touching, and I think, absurdly, *I'm caught in the act*. But before I can even ask myself, *Caught in the act of what, for godsake?* he reaches into the pocket of his parka, pulls out a brass bell with a black wooden handle, and rings it in between us on the street corner as the twilight sets in.

"You wanna buy this bell? You could get twenty bucks for it in one of those antique stores down that way on Queen. I just don't feel like walking. I been walking all day and night. I just wanna buy myself a meal. All I've had is a donut," he says, still ringing the bell. It's the kind teachers used to have sitting on oak desks, once upon a time.

I shake my head as if from a spell and say, "No. No, I don't need a bell." But I give him a two-dollar coin, pick it out from among the pennies and nickels that came up when I stuck my hand into the pocket of my grandfather's coat.

"Can I have that too?" he asks, pointing to my fist as I go to return the change to my pocket. I'm usually quick to draw the line when somebody gets pushy, but this guy has an artlessness about him that disarms me. His hand, outstretched, is shaking. I nod and dump the change into his outstretched palm. He pockets it along with the bell.

"You sure you can't spare some more?" he asks, aware, I guess, that he's caught a live one.

I say, "No, that's all I've got," even though I've got a twenty in my wallet and am on my way to more shopping. As usual, I'm now on to the next layer of it all—starting to feel more sheepish about my middle class guilt than my middle class privilege. We part ways and I don't look back, just squirm inwardly and wish, in spite of myself, that I hadn't spent almost a whole night of tips on the satchel.

I meet him again about fifteen minutes later as I'm coming out of the hardware store with a little yellow plastic bag holding a newly cut key and a very good quality can opener that I don't strictly need but that will make opening cans a much more pleasant experience. He opens his mouth to ask me for change, then recognizes me and says, "Hey, don't I know you?" I smile genuinely, more at myself than anything. At my awareness of the yellow bag—caught in the act again. He doesn't even glance at my purchases, just steers me off to the inside edge of the sidewalk and leans in toward me almost as if confiding—though a little ominously as well.

"Hey," he says, "you sure you can't spare any more? It's a good bell, look nice on the mantel." He gives it a little ring, just above his pocket, and cocks his head. For a second I'm not sure if I'm being mocked—am figuring, *Yeah, probably I'm being mocked*—when he leans in and says softly, "I just wanna get something to eat. You sure you can't spare any more? It's bad panhandling around here. I could go down to the banks at King and Dufferin and panhandle there, but I've been walking all day and all night."

Nodding, almost nauseous with the cocktail of compassion, shame and rattled annoyance (at him and at myself), I open the satchel to rummage for my wallet. I give him another two-dollar coin, even though I still have a five. I offer him an apple that I have, too, regretting it the moment I do, the wholesome condescension of it.

He says, "Naw, I don't eat apples," and then he says, "You're a nice woman, you married?" I roll my eyes and start walking. "Yeah," he calls after me, "I should have known it—I woulda jumped on you too." Is he nodding at my effort, thanking me for giving more than most, just trying to have some casual human contact, or subtly asserting the only power he has over me? Probably—no, definitely—all of the above. I hear him walk off down the sidewalk behind me in the other direction for about ten paces, then stop and yell, "Hey."

I turn to face him, ready to be firm, but he just waves again.

I wave back—and that's it.

It's not until a moment later, as I jaywalk across the street, that it occurs to me, I could have bought the bell. It would have been nice to have. On my mantel, even. It didn't have to be a rip-off. It could have been an exchange. Twenty bucks for a constant reminder. Though of what, I couldn't exactly tell you.

❧

Funny enough, it wasn't the killing that did it. Wasn't whole families being bayonetted in their beds. Or Father being shot. Tried putting my finger on it in the years since and finally figured it: the lack of foresight was what really shook me. Shook *us*.

You might say that's mighty advanced—a boy all shaken up by a lack of foresight, but what you don't understand is children were a different breed then. Whole other animals. More serious. More expected of them. Especially the eldest boy in a family of six and no father.

I suppose I took my cue from Mother. Watching her eyes watch the bread. Always aware how many days worth of bread we had left, how much dried fruit. We measured food in days and let me tell you we were experts in calculating the stretch of it in seven mouths with seven different limits as to how much hunger they could tolerate before they'd cry out or their legs give out from under them. There's a saying: *What bread really is, only the hungry man knows.*

The food would have to stretch even further when the bands of looters came through, moving in and boarding with us for weeks at a time. Soldiers they called themselves. The Reds one week, Whites the next. Then the Anarchists. They all looked the same to us children, and I remember Mother whispering, *Different leaders, same appetites.* I remember the look in Mother's eyes the time they slaughtered our cow right when she was about to calf just because they had a hankering for a roast of meat. They'd kill all the chickens and still be wanting eggs. And winter just around the corner. And when a neighbour came with the news that the men staying with them had taken to sawing off the rafters of their house for firewood, Mother didn't say anything, just raised her chin and pressed her lips together and looked aside. Great blazing fires and those men in their undershirts with their feet up like there was no tomorrow. And then they began to cut down the pear and cherry trees in the communal orchard for firewood as well. All those years of dried fruit and me watching Mother's knuckles whiten as she wrung the soldiers' laundry, her back to their fire.

❧

Remember how frustrating it can be to sit in traffic in rush hour and have no control over how fast you can move or when you will get to your destination?

Did you ever take a vacation in a country where you did not understand the language and you had difficulty communicating with the people around you? Imagine the problem being compounded by the use of a different alphabet, such as Hebrew, Arabic, Greek or Russian.

Have you ever watched a movie with a very complicated plot and had a lot of difficulty following it? Have you ever walked into a movie halfway through, or turned on a television show when it was half over, and not known who the characters were or how they related to each other?

❧

Stuck in traffic on the westbound streetcar I close my eyes
and drift, somersault backwards into warm waters, summers
at the house on Silver Street: the world map wallpaper in
the guest room, the pucker of gooseberries in my cheeks,
Grandpa's drawer full of shoehorns, harmonicas and pipes,
the cousins in the covered pool in the backyard, the inflatable
canoe. We were always on the brink of having all the leaks
patched, always on the cusp of having it float. We struggled
inside it as it hissed—shrinking, sinking—paddled for all we
were worth, wanting to get in some movement across before
the down took over.

I settle on Grandma. On Mary Friesen and whoever's in
her head, pulling it apart like a small closet stuffed with forty
years of clothing and she's looking for that burnt-leather belt
that Ruth made for Dad in 4-H and little Nick borrowed
for Halloween 1959 (cowboy, of course). In the evening she
is going through her closet as Grandpa sits in the darkened
kitchen with his head in his hands, elbows resting on the
table that once had farmhands chewing and *yes-ma'am*-ing
around it, failing sturdily in their efforts to be polite. She
goes methodically through her closet. It's time

for bed. She hasn't turned on the light so squints. It's time

for bed, so she takes off the clothes that he dressed her in this
morning—the bra he fastened with cracked fingertips, the
pantyhose he insisted upon. She goes through the narrow
closet beside the bed, puts on the grey woollen dress,

the one with the red belt
can't reach the zipper

Christmas 1968.

She pulls back the covers that she straightened this morning
in a comfortable interlude of habit. She sits down on the bed,
swings her legs up, leans back. No need to turn out the light.
It's already dark. Backwards somersault into dark water

a deepening closet

bare V of her unzipped back against the bedspread,

an arrow of elegance in disorientation.

I'm tipping backwards over and over again in the covered
pool in the backyard. The sun goes down. The patio lanterns
are switched on. I continue, water up my nose, body tucked,
arms out, fingers pressed close, symmetrical. Hands efficient
fins round and round in small circles, propelling my form,
surrounded by the sound of the world slowed down. I love
to dive in and be slowed. I am utterly at home underneath,
the world gone slow, sound gone swollen. I will have water
in my ears. Inside, Grandpa with his elbows on the table,
head in hands, Grandma trying to remember which way is
backwards, gratefully remembering that wool is warm.

꙳

One of my showers is a burly, brain-injured man in his forties or fifties named Fred. Too young to be here, but where else are they going to put him, I guess. "Motorcycle accident," says Barb. Hard to tell how much he understands. He uses clichés and catchphrases, repeats them with uncanny appropriateness. "Time will tell," he kept saying to me my first night. "Patience is a virtue."

Whenever I ask him how he wants something done— whether he wants to wear slippers to the shower room, whether he feels he can dry himself off—he says with what feels like a stubborn and sage ambiguity, "You enlighten me."

Hard to say where injury stops and humour begins.

〜

My grandfather does not have fishing stories; he has injury stories. He collects them.

There is, for instance, a whole set of broken arm stories: the time he was examining the chimney and the ladder fell, and the one when Uncle Nick fell from a tree during an ambush while playing Cowboys and Indians (the branch snapped—*Two limbs broken in one go*, Grandpa used to say). And of course there's the one where the boy tripped Grandpa with his hockey stick when Grandma had her class out to skate on the irrigation pond. Not to mention the famous lesson Grandpa taught the boy. That time he broke his wrist so thoroughly his hand flopped against his forearm and, if I have it right, the only available doctor was drunk and set the bone wrong and it had to be rebroken a few months later.

It seems to me they were always breaking their arms so hard their bones came through the skin.

And it wasn't just broken arms. Sprains, concussions, missing fingers, bleeding noses, dislocated shoulders. Accidents, fights. Bravery and foolhardiness of all kinds. Farmhands, relatives, friends, neighbouring farmers, adults, children—all were swollen, bruised and bloody.

Then they sold the farm and he went to nursing school, and there were more stories. His first job was nurse at the Massey Ferguson plant. A man's hand was cut off in the machinery one day, blood everywhere. While everyone else was panicking Grandpa stayed calm, made a good tourniquet, slowed the blood until the ambulance came. There was a Red Cross blood donor clinic across the way at the Legion Hall that day, but none of the boys had the stomach for it. They closed the plant and everyone went home early—except Grandpa. He unwrapped his ham sandwich from its waxed paper and strolled on over to give blood.

"Peter stop telling stories like that at the dinner table," Grandma would chime in.

"Always had a strong stomach," he'd say to me. "Now eat that horseradish. It'll put hair on your chest."

Today we're in the workshop. Grandpa's telling James the story of the irrigation-pond-hockey-stick incident. My back turned, I'm flipping through seed packets, fingering the dried basil and dill hanging from the rafters. Grandpa launches into the story of the apple tree and Nick's broken arm and the drunken doctor from Fergus. James laughs in all the right places, scoffs appropriately, is manly but sufficiently amazed and at the same time manages to avoid effusiveness or undue enthusiasm. There's a subtle, unspoken scorn in the air for men with soft handshakes.

When James reaches absently across the sawhorse to rub the small of my back, I flinch and move away towards the wall where my old red wagon is hanging. He doesn't seem to notice, continues listening to Grandpa, hooting at the circumstances of the concussion on Christmas Eve 1956, Santa Claus costume and all. His hand, lacking my back, is now wandering over the tools on the counter. He picks up an old set of wooden clamps, weighing them with a kind of entitlement entirely foreign to me, and for a moment I'm no longer sure about anything.

❧

James and I have been together seven years, going on eight.

When we met, we fell instantly for each other's instinctive earnestness, because it meant that our own—which was embarrassing out of doors, in public—could have company. We had a shared suspicion of technology, a shared awe for the concept of the vow. He was a practising Catholic, and this freaked me out until he assured me that he was also an anarchist.

"Nietzsche didn't have any particular problem with Jesus," he said. "It was Christians he couldn't stand."

On our second date we went to an anti-NAFTA protest. I remember someone was carrying a huge banner that said, DOWN WITH THE CONTENTED.

He quoted Whitman to me: *Do I contradict myself? Very well then, I contradict myself. I am large. I contain multitudes.* I quoted back: *As the child sees the world the world is.* We knew everything.

Who can ever say exactly what makes us open to another person? Chance, uncanny passwords. I remember a cartoon torn from a newspaper. He'd tacked it to the ulcerous, uncleanable, paint-flaking, layer-a-tenant wall beside his bathroom mirror. It was an image of people mingling at a cocktail party. A huge thought bubble hovered over the crowd, fed by little tributaries of bubbles from each person's head. Inside the bubble, this thought: *Everyone's having a good time but me.* It made me trust him.

Squalls of irritation: sitting at the kitchen table together, him reading the paper, me making notes on a book for a course I'm taking and my pen is running out of ink and he's chewing his yogurt (who the hell *chews* yogurt?) and it's all I can do to keep from stuffing my pen up his nose.

Moments of intense seeing: watching him swim alone in an Algonquin Park lake one autumn afternoon, something about the sight of him treading water way out—his back to me, the sky darkening above—makes me want nothing more than to love him well.

"Can there be any love without pity?" A couple of years ago I came across this line in a novel and, even though it was a question rather than a statement, I remember feeling absolved by it somehow. Absolved of a crime I hadn't quite known I suspected myself of having committed.

His father was a violent man, and this means that James is awkwardly tender, a tinman afraid he didn't inherit a heart. There's an ache in his eyes that makes them look constantly astonished. When we met, I quickly became addicted to giving him a new reason for that astonishment. It was like facing a man who's falling backward; if you catch his outstretched hands and immediately fall backward with all *your* weight, both of your falls are transformed into the first gesture of a dance.

We were introduced by friends one night and within five days we'd pooled all our money. We moved in together within three weeks. We gave the biggest coin we had between us to every beggar and busker we passed. We married—just the two of us at city hall—within the year. I was nineteen and he was twenty-four.

"Babies!" his landlady snorted derisively. "I wasn't smart enough to choose my own underwear when I was nineteen."

But she gave us a wedding present anyway: an "Instant Romance" kit from Zellers, which consisted of a bottle of sparkling wine, a pair of fake crystal champagne flutes and a matching candle holder. We drank it on the roof of the building, spreading a blanket over the pigeon shit so we could lie down and look at the stars.

Married at nineteen in this day and age. I thought I'd found a shortcut. To what though? I didn't have a clear idea, but intuited a strenuousness, a muscularity, both noble and animal, in the notion of mating for life.

Or maybe it was just a kind of RRSP of the heart.

༄

Sometimes he sets her up to do the dishes when he needs a break. That works for a while, but then it gets to the point where she's just washing the same plate over and over and over and over until he simply can't stand it any longer.

I was there last week when it happened. Grandpa got up, snatched the plate from her, dashed it to the floor and sat down again, all in one motion.

I held my breath, eyes on a triangle of china near my foot. It was from the edge of the plate. Gold trim. Apple blossom pattern. The good china on the farm, demoted to everyday china when they got the Denby pattern after they moved to town.

My breath ran out. He let go his fist, pushed his chair back and walked unsteadily to the side door. Didn't look at either of us, let the screen door slam behind him.

I was free to look at her then. Her lips were twitching slightly, as if searching for their rightful shape. After a while they settled in an apologetic smile, and she tugged her eyes from the window, rested them on me. All I could think to do was the other thing that Grandpa always does lately when he needs a rest from her. I steered her around the broken plate, out of the kitchen, into the front room. Guided her down onto the piano stool. Opened the songbook. "Tie a Yellow Ribbon."

Standing behind her, I placed her hands on the keys, pulled the chain on the lamp and set the metronome swinging.

She looked back at me; I nodded.

She looked at the music.

She pressed the first chord: dissonance.

She tried again: again, a random, jarring blare. She looked back at me.

"It's okay," I said, trying to make my smile mild—a balm, a sling. I pointed my eyes to the keys. "Try again."

So she played.

Had she missed the flats? She didn't stop. Was she playing in the wrong key? She didn't stop. Had she started with her hands in the wrong position?

The roof was falling in. She didn't stop.

When she came to the end of the music her hands slipped off the keys into her lap, but she kept her foot on the pedal, letting the room steep briefly in the sound of the wrong notes, sustained.

~

First time I saw my own bone was when we had the farm. Mary had coaxed me into clearing the irrigation pond to make a rink. Wanted to have her class out for a Christmas skating party. I did, and it was a hit alright. The kids were pretty wound up, and near dark one of the boys thought he was being smart and tripped me with his hockey stick as I was skating by. Well I went flying, and when I hit the ice my forearm snapped—you could hear the sound of it clear as anything in the cold air, just like kindling snapped over your knee. Shot clear through the skin. Well I taught that lad a lesson he'd never forget. I got myself seated in the snowbank and then told him to hold his stick out crosswise. I put my loose hand on the stick, put my good hand over it and yelled at him, *Pull goddammit!* And by golly he pulled. His face like a popsicle with all the colour sucked from it. Together we got that bone back in place until I could get myself to a doctor.

I'll never forget that, the sight of my own bone in the open air. The thought of it could get to you, if you let it.

~

Monday morning. I walk to work. I've taken a day shift at the bar as a favour to someone who recently did me a favour (in this way the economy of the bar keeps going—we all drink there and overtip each other, a potlatch battle to be the one to buy the drinks).

I hate day shifts. It's quiet and relaxed and you make decent money 'cause there's no one to tip out and the weekday afternoon drinkers all tip well (that nucleus of regulars who all make their livings in canny, shifty ways—musicians, bouncers and landlords on disability, a comedian, a chef, guys who maybe gamble or deal a little on the side), but it's depressing. I hate having to watch how the first shot-and-beer-chaser of the day steadies the hands of certain paper-reading regulars.

A woman stands on the corner of King and Dowling. She's wearing a loose Simpsons t-shirt, bicycle shorts and black pumps with a low heel, almost demure. Nothing exactly advertising sex, except maybe the shoes, but her hip is cocked into the street with such hook, such unmasked intention, that there's no room to think she might just be waiting for a cab or a streetcar. Passing her, giving her a wide berth so as not to disturb the charged ring she's conjuring around herself, I see for a second how hard the work is. Pouring oneself out into bottomless streets.

꙳

Liza can't remember where her washcloths are kept or how the aloe plant got into the basket of her walker, but she teases me so skillfully as I wash her back that I can imagine just how she flirted with her now-dead husband the year they were both working at a summer camp and fell for each other. She was in the kitchen, he was the maintenance man. She was almost thirty then, and I imagine she'd given up on all that, considered herself an old maid. I imagine he woke a dormant rascal in her. I imagine their romance involved threading worms onto hooks and sunlight and swimming.

The other day Liza was late for dinner because she got halfway to the dining hall and realized she was barefoot, had to shuffle back to her room for her shoes and socks.

Her feet are ticklish. They jump as I wash them.

Last night she told me a joke as I helped her off with her clothes—a joke about a truck driver picking up a hitchhiking little girl and asking her to take off her pants and the girl giggling 'cause there was no way her pants would fit that man. Liza laughed then sobered. "It's not fair," she said to me, "you all dressed and me naked."

She said it so plainly that for a moment, I had a genuine impulse to take off my clothes.

∾

The Russian formalist literary theorists have this word I love. *Ostranenie*. It translates more or less as defamiliarization. To tilt things at such an angle that we can see them new, beyond the patina bestowed by habit. Often the goal is to reveal a horror or hypocrisy we've become used to. Or to reveal a beauty we take for granted. Sometimes the goal is even more elusive—to steal a glimpse of the essential hard-to-get-at strangeness of being here at all.

Which, I think, is maybe the seat of beauty. I'm in the reference library photocopying an out-of-print book of philosophy for James for his birthday. He's been looking for it for ages. It's called, *On Science, Necessity and the Love of God*. In my hands is the only copy in the entire Toronto Public Library system. I've phoned all the second-hand bookstores in the city so know there aren't any copies there. I found one for sale on the internet, but it was a first edition in mint condition and out of my price range. I have to admit I'm enjoying the feeling of photocopying a rare, out-of-print book. Makes me feel special. Nothing wrong with that; nothing special about wanting to feel special.

I keep having to fend people off when they stand behind me waiting for the copier. *I'll be a while*, I say calmly, over my shoulder. *I'm copying the whole book*. The people pause then wander off, bewildered to find they have no recourse.

The reference library is a grand, stadium-like building with five high-ceilinged open-concept floors arranged in rings around a cavernous centre space. I stand at a photocopy machine on the third floor, looking out over the hushed library, its rings. People of every race and creed, each of them on a mission—to do the research for their political science essay, to find out about the rash in their crotch, to extend their family tree, to pass the afternoon quietly in the presence of other human beings.

I think of Dante, his rings.

Of my Buddhist friend Gloria who says she thinks the hell realms are here on earth, and we all go in and out of them.

I lift the lid, turn the page, close the lid, press the button.

Two young Asian girls in a corner on the first floor are practising the slow movements of some martial art, taking turns, whispering modifying instructions to one another.

I lift, turn, close, press.

Tonight in the bath I will read Simone Weil on quantum physics by candlelight. James is away again—a few shows up north. I'll take the portable phone into the bathroom with me in case he calls from the road and when he does he'll say I can't understand a word you're saying, it sounds like you're under water.

When I'm finished photocopying I ride my bike home westward into the sun, squinting. People waiting at street corners keep smiling at me. After a while I realize that my face squinting must look like it's smiling, beaming in fact. Through no fault of my own, completely by accident, I've been riding through the city making people smile. The sun so directly in my eyes I can only make out shapes, not details of the cars ahead. Probably not even safe to be riding.

A wave of strangeness takes me; it's one-part time, one-part eternity, one-part secret ingredient. It comes to me that fear of death is, from another angle, love of the world. The desire not to be excluded from the world. That perhaps at the heart of all my miscellaneous fear is the assumption that after death I will stop being a part of things. I stand on my pedals and coast westward along Queen.

～

Barb is very strict with the residents about their scheduled showers and baths. They get washed whether they feel like it or not. At first I thought her unfeeling, even cruel. But gradually you see what she's up against. Somebody has to make sure the old people don't smell. And if I don't shower Mavis tonight, the morning girl will have to do it on top of the forty beds she has to strip and the round of meds she has to give. When a resident declines emphatically enough though, Barb sometimes acquiesces. She'll sigh then and say to me, "Why don't you go get Henry and do the halls?"

Henry is the vacuum cleaner—a squat red thing on wheels with decals of eyes on either side of the hose. I pull it along the hallway by the nose, smiling at residents, raising a hand, nodding. Some of them ask me how my boyfriend is today, meaning Henry. I'll have to think of a witty response. I'm not very good at the witty response.

I am, however, starting to think I might be good at radiating warmth. Mavis today, for instance: when she didn't answer my knock, I let myself into her room to ask when she wanted her shower. She's been reluctant to have her showers lately. When I stepped in, she was sitting on the side of her bed staring at the wall as if waiting for a portal to open up and take her away. I sat down beside her and chatted for a while. She was slow to respond, as if scared to trust that my warmth was genuine and wouldn't be snatched away the moment she began to lean on it.

On the way home that night, I caught myself calculating that, if I worked the extra job another six months, my student loans would be paid off and I could quit.

Mavis and Barb are right to be suspicious.

Imagine that you are sitting with a group of old friends. In the middle of the conversation you start to daydream, when suddenly you hear someone saying to you, "What do you think about that?" Or think back to when you were part of a group of three or four people who were having a wide-ranging conversation for a half hour or so. Suddenly, someone said, "How did we get onto this topic, anyway?" Did the question disturb you?

❧

We drive, the four of us—me, Mom, Grandma and Grandpa—in the old Plymouth, the car rattling and jolting, my forehead shivering against the window. I have a vague image of cogs under the hood, large watch-like parts and, to account for the rattling, something coming loose, something no longer connecting on its way around with the other things on their way around. Grandma counts the cows in the passing fields and tells the car of cranky adults that there are six of them. One. Two. Three. Four. Five. Then she asks me for the fourth time if I live with some nice girls, and I lie to her for the fourth time and say, "Yes Grandma, I live with some nice girls."

Grandma's met James, of course, but her decline was already well underway by the time he came around. As far as I know, she's been officially informed of neither our marriage nor our co-habitation; I think Mom figured the thought of a wedding she hadn't been invited to would be almost as bad to Grandma as the thought of her granddaughter living in sin. And besides, what would be the point when she wouldn't retain the information anyway?

I turn and press my forehead against the cool glass of the window again, as Grandpa slowly, ever-so-slowly tells how Mom and Uncle Nick used to skate to school on that creek. We pass the one-room schoolhouse (now with a deck and a two-car garage), and Mom tells how on days when the weather was too harsh to go outside, the kids would spend recess in the basement by the wood-burning furnace, jumping over the logs. The car rounds the corner of their old farm. I remind myself that I asked for this. I wanted to see the particular roll of these fields, the angles of the farmhouse roof against the sky.

Yes Grandma, I live with some nice girls. What if it's not just the disease that keeps her coming back to the question? What if some untamed element in her is hell-bent of late, hollowed by urgency, hungry for what is. *Yes Grandma, I live with some nice girls.* The taming instinct handed down, in skewed relay, to me.

We turn up the long driveway, and I close my eyes—the sound of gravel under slowly rolling tires, a farm dog barking from the porch. "Something's different," Mom says, then gasps. "They took off the gable where my bedroom used to be, took it right off." Grandpa says that the bright green kilns have a fresh coat of paint, but they're the same old kilns alright. The old irrigation pond is gone, filled in, but the oak tree in the yard is still there, even grander now. I watch Grandma. She blinks. Mom does a three-point turn, and that's it.

On the way out we pass a tiny white clapboard house on the far corner of the farm, a curly pattern in the aluminum of the screen door, the windows boarded up with plywood. "That's the house where Mother lived," Grandpa says reverently, as if it were the childhood home of a great artist or statesman.

I close my eyes and see the work-battered hands of Great-Grandma Helena Friesen. She lived in that little house all the time Mom was growing up. I know the stories like my own neighbourhood. Mom used to round the corner on her way home from school, ready to spend the afternoon with Great-Grandma and her huge, cracked fingers teaching needlework while the radio crackled out its soap operas. Needlework was a guilty pleasure for her; Mennonites saw it as frivolous.

In my mind every afternoon Mom rounds the corner and Great-Grandma is there—in her overalls because she is gardening, a dress over top of them because she is a woman, a large white bandage wrapped again and again around her head for her migraines and a babushka on top of it all.

I try to think what in the world Great-Grandma would have thought of frivolous me. Poetry, for godsake.

Grandma's hand closes even more tightly around mine, and I glance at her profile. Her eyes are closed. I try to picture what's going on in her head. A little girl rounding some corner, rounding it and rounding it again.

What'll I be like when I'm her age? Sometimes a thought doesn't bear thinking. Like serving a piece of a pie that hasn't set, it slips off the lifter when you try to pick it up.

&

Peter Friesen, the bachelor who works the Dowswell farm, has been paying me visits. Mrs. McKinnon becomes terribly excited when she sees him pulling his team into the drive. She's begun referring to him as *the teacher's beau*, which I think is rather hasty and more than a little alarming. Of course he's nice in his way, but he has been all over and is not what one would call the settled sort. I have always said I didn't want to be a farmer's wife. However, one thing does stand out—Mr. Peter Friesen has begun to attend the Presbyterian Church. Fancy that. *You can always give an old dog new spots*, he said to me Sunday evening when he took me out for a drive. Isn't that dear? Oh he's nice enough, but as far as I'm concerned I have not chosen to be Mrs. Peter Friesen. Somehow I can't help feeling though that simply by not saying no to his friendly gestures and to the invitations of others who invite the two of us on the same day to their homes, I am consenting by increments to something larger.

Is that how one gets married? Not so much by saying yes as by not saying no?

❦

"I don't know why people think they can pursue happiness directly anyway. It doesn't work that way," James says. He's back from his tour and we're celebrating his birthday with a bottle of wine on the steps of the front porch. Streetlights on. My head in his lap.

"What do you mean?"

"I mean happiness is a by-product. Happiness is beside the point."

"What is the point then?"

"I don't know. Doing right by people. Becoming really good at one or two things. Noticing shit."

"And if you do those things—living right—then you'll be happy on the side?"

"No, not necessarily. Not exactly. No guarantees."

"No guarantees?"

"Nope. No guarantees."

"Promise?"

I shift my head from his lap and look up at him.

"I do," he says.

~

On Friday night during the busiest part of the evening the cops crept up the back fire escape and did a surprise "takedown" in the apartment above the bar, a manoeuvre complete with deafening stun-grenade to blast open the door, the whole crowd below ducking expertly at the sound, pints in hand. As far as anyone can figure, the man who'd been renting the apartment had been gradually befriended and usurped and, over a period of weeks or months, the place had become an actual instance of that infamous thing: a crackhouse.

Apparently the day after the takedown a woman called the police saying she'd been locked out of her apartment. The cops came in the middle of the brunch rush and started hassling Roxanne about it. Roxanne is the owner of the bar and landlord of the apartment. She dried her hands on her apron and said, "Uh, maybe you boys should talk to your friends back at the station about the takedown they did last night upstairs?"

The cops looked flustered and went back out to their car. Meanwhile, a wiry woman on the sidewalk screamed at their backs, "I know my rights you fuckers." You've got to admire the guts.

Roxanne can't get her insurance company to pay for the damage to the apartment because her rates would skyrocket to the point of putting her out of business, so today a bunch of the staff—me, Leona, Sammy and Ursula—gather to clean out the apartment. The new manager is going to move in.

The smell is the first thing. Surely the only way such

a reek could have accumulated would be if people were peeing directly on the plywood floors. We stand huddled in the middle of the room for a few minutes, rotating as if surrounded by a hostile force: stained and sheetless mattresses listing off the sides of equally stained box springs; matching couch and armchair, a light grey with greasy darker grey patches on the armrests, impossible to tell their original colour; everywhere you look, bulky black stereo equipment, obsolete, unplugged, forlorn; in one corner some stacks of hardcover books, a stubborn lump of order not yet dissolved into the generalized chaos; in the kitchen sink a half-inch of bloated rice in a watery reddish sauce; Stouffer's TV dinner boxes inexplicably stapled around the kitchen door frame; the floor carpeted with newspapers, plastic bags, lone socks, cutlery, flimsy towels, coat hangers, an argyle sweater, a broken-off chair-leg, ashtrays, pocket change, candle stubs, tinfoil. And over it all, debris from ceiling tiles the police broke in their adrenalin-charged search for drugs—that and a sense of intensified gravity.

Finally someone strides forward, tears the black garbage bags off the front windows, and we set to, trying not to think too much about how this happens to a life.

Leona runs downstairs and brings up the snow shovel we use in winter to scrape the sidewalk in front of the bar, goes at the kitchen floor with it. I pull on a pair of brand new bright yellow rubber gloves and begin randomly stuffing things into a garbage bag. Sammy holds it open for me. A drawerful of sealed syringes. A little mountain of condom packages and breathmint samples spilling off the coffee table. A pair of black pumps with a slight heel, barely scuffed. "Crackwhore kit," says Sammy, pointing. Then, "Sorry, black humour."

The radio's on. We all begin to find a rhythm in the work.

A mostly empty notebook with a list of *Favourite Character Actors* in the front and an impenetrable and meticulous series of numbers and tiny Xs filling five whole pages in the back, as if the owner had been compelled to keep score for some relentless and sinister game. A sample pack of six sardine tins—lemon, jalapeno, tomato, mustard, jerk and original—wrapped in cellophane and tied with a curling red ribbon. A file of clippings from the *Toronto Sun*: POWs in Lebanon, plane crash off Peggy's Cove, death of Trudeau, scandals and natural disasters, the file reading like research for a definitive document detailing the varieties of upheaval.

On the radio a smarmy-voiced ad for a mutual fund. Someone calls out, "Does this station ever play music?" Someone else goes over and turns the dial.

At one point Roxanne comes out of the bathroom doing a little dance and singing, "Look what the cops missed and I found!" A baggie of pot in a little brown velvet jewellery case.

Altogether we collect enough change for a two-four. We also find two crackpipes made from gluesticks. But we all agree that the prize for best find has to go to Ursula, who found the pin to the stun grenade.

We take a break. As we clink our beer bottles, Sammy says, "Having friends is better than having insurance any day."

On the radio a blues song crossed with a high and keening native chant. Aboriginal Voices 96.1 FM.

The canned food and books and some of the less offensive

furniture we put out on the street for passersby to take. The rest we throw off the fire escape into the restaurant dumpster out back. After we've been working for a couple of hours, I look out the front window onto the sidewalk below. A small crowd has gathered around the free stuff, many of them with open books in their hands as if attending an impromptu study group. I watch an older man in a faded jean jacket choose *Robert's Rules of Order* and *Introduction to Modern Behaviorism*, slip them into his shopping bag along with the sardines and ride off on his bicycle.

For a prolonged and disquieting moment when I turn back to the room, everything—diminishing piles of debris, armchair on its side as if it's passed out, my own hand on the windowsill, even the reeking air itself—everything seems to bind together into a thick quivering whole as if by chemical reaction, some kind of gelatin in the day that, having been stirred and stirred, has finally taken. I stand there by the window, immobilized.

Then, just as quickly, the elements of the room unbind themselves from each other and fall back, spent, separate after all.

When we're done, I take off my rubber gloves, plucking each fingertip loose like a lady at a ball.

mary mary

☙

from *Mind Your Manners: A Complete Dictionary of Etiquette for Canadians*

appointments: Be on time.
(found after lengthy entries for *apology* and *applause*)

personal questions: Never ask any.
(found between a cryptic entry on *perfume* and an entry under the heading of *pineapple* which explains the proper use of cutlery at luncheons)

~

I phoned Mother one Sunday
she phoned me the next

I phoned her one Sunday
she phoned me the next

I phoned her one Sunday
she phoned me the next

෫

I'm not sure if it was Grandpa or Mom and Uncle Nick who made the decision. Whatever the case, it certainly wasn't Grandma.

There isn't much to move really. Or much to say. It's a hot, awkward afternoon. Mom takes charge, arranging the bright track suits in the little closet beside the bed, pointing things out to the nurse on duty, asking questions about meal times and laundry routines.

Uncle Nick volunteers to walk the block and a half back to the house to fetch a hammer and nail so we can hang the family picture above the narrow bed. I envy him: twenty minutes in the place and I'm craving fresh air. The "Retirement Home" I work at, with its private rooms and ploys at homeyness, is much less depressing than the Extended Care section of this nursing home—the residents here much further along in the continuum of decline. Part of me is wishing one of my cousins had come so we could sneak out together for a cigarette, though part of me is also feeling a little smug being the only one of my generation to have shown up.

Grandpa speaks only to Grandma, and only in short commands. "Stop that," he barks when she begins to chew loudly on nothing. When she wanders over to the other side of the room and starts to make one of the other ladies' beds, he lets out a sharp, "Leave it." After that he steers her to the vinyl bench by the window and sits there beside her, keeping a tight grip on her hand.

Mom's big discovery of the afternoon is that they still have a piano in the lounge. She brightens. "Look Dad, she'll be able to practise. We'll have to bring her sheet music over. I wonder how we can keep it from getting lost." Already fishing through her purse for her notepad so she can add *sheet music for Mom* to her list.

When it comes time to go Mom put her hands on her knees with a slap and stands up. We all take the cue. "Well," she says, "I guess we'd better get going." She pauses. "You're going to stay here Mum. Remember how we talked about this?"

Grandma is on her feet, having risen with the rest of us at the signal to leave. Now Grandpa walks over to her side, takes her elbow and guides her to sit down on the bed. "This is where you'll sleep now, Mary."

Grandma looks at each of us in turn, her mouth slightly open. She settles on Grandpa. "But I want to go with you," she says.

Mom sits down on her other side and points to the family picture that Uncle Nick has hung. "See Mum, there's the family and—"

"I want to go with you," she says to Grandpa, her voice rising.

Grandpa takes her hand and looks at the ceiling for a moment before looking at her. When he speaks his voice is firm, almost harsh. "You have to stay here Mary," he says, "and we have to go."

Then I witness a barely perceptible shift in her face. Her chin lifts. Her breathing slows. It's as if she's found reins. I don't think it's that she's understood. I think it's something subtler than that, something to do with the long practice of rising to the occasion. It's as if she's felt a familiar tug—the imperative of not making a scene in public perhaps, or maybe just the sheer habit of doing what needs to be done. She pulls herself together.

After all, who's going to do it if she doesn't?

~

That sound—the creak of the line through the pulley when I'm hanging out the wash—always puts me in mind of the farm. Peter had strung up a clothesline between the house and the oak tree in the side yard. My favourite chore was hanging out the laundry in the morning there under that tree. Time by myself, thinking about what needed doing and what was already done. What needed doing and what was already done. Shirts and pants and sheets and aprons. Half of them hung out to dry—stretching their arms and legs in the wind, I liked to think—and half of them bunched in the basket, waiting to be hung. The creak of the line through the pulley. What needed doing and what was already done and then later that afternoon pulling the line back in the other direction, the clothes stiff and dry and good-smelling. Filling the hamper. Ironing next. The line between what needed doing and what was already done going back and forth all the time, things building up on one side then the other like a see-saw. It takes a steady woman to keep up with it on a farm, all that back and forth. Let me tell you.

ॐ

things that have left her:

1 first, her ability to remember

(then to wonder) whether she already asked
you the question she's been meaning
to ask you

2 pride
about her false teeth

3 bladder control

4 her tendency to comment on stains
and fallen hems and showing slips and
holes in socks

5 her ability to knit

and crochet and embroider and
mend

6 her disdain for beer

Grandpa feeds it to her often now, and I can't decide
whether it's revenge or a sort of tenderness,
making up for lost
time

7 names

in this order: the names
of her acquaintances and of her neighbours; the names
of her curling friends, choir friends, old teaching friends;
the name
of the United Church minister and of the little boy
with Down's syndrome who came every week to swim in
the pool; the names
of her grandchildren her husband her children and lately
her own names both married and
maiden

❧

Lois King, interim treasurer, United Church Women (UCW), Branch 186, St. James United Church, Paris, Ontario

Oh, Mary was always showing the rest of us up. I'll admit I even felt a little peeved at her from time to time. Seems so silly now, what with... well, you know. Oh but *then*. If it was a beautiful spring day and you said to yourself what the heck and wore your new white shoes to church even a day before the 24th of May, well. You could tell she noticed. Not that she would say anything of course, but her eyes would go straight to your shoes and then she'd shake your husband's hand but wouldn't stay to chat. *Lois,* John always used to say to me, *Lois, if you didn't have anything to worry about you'd have to invent something. It's just your imagination,* he'd say. *Aren't you the one always saying she's your best friend?* he'd say. *Yes yes,* I'd say, *but that doesn't mean she can't be a pain in the neck sometimes.* There were her thank-you notes for instance. She was positively *renowned* for her thank-you notes. She had a system, and she didn't mind telling you about it either. Whenever she was invited to a dinner or a tea or a luncheon or a shower or any kind of party or gathering, she'd make out the envelope beforehand, address it and stamp it, get it all ready to go. Then the moment she got home from the outing she'd write the thank-you note easy as pie from some formula Lord knows she must have carried around in her very *bones,* and then she'd seal it and stick it in the mailbox that very evening, neat as can be. Beyond reproach. Couldn't touch her. Not Mary.

No, I don't think I was imagining anything. Though that doesn't mean I don't miss her like the dickens. Things aren't the same in the UCW, that much is for sure. You could always count on Mary.

ॐ

When she'd start in on one of her stories all of us kids—the cousins and I—we'd drop our forks, roll our eyes and kick each other under the table.

Her favourite was the one about the fiancée of their best farmhand. Grandma would tell this story whenever our table manners slipped, whenever we bent our bodies the least bit toward our forks instead of bringing our forks—properly— to our mouths.

In the old days on the farm during harvest, they all ate at the same table with the crew. And this woman, the farmhand's fiancée—she must have been working in the curing house—would roll up her sleeves, push her chair back, and bend over so low that she could get the food into her mouth without lifting her arm. Apparently she held her fork wrong too, held it straight out in her fist—*Like a savage,* Grandma said. Or sometimes, her voice rich with disbelief, she'd exclaim, *Just like a baby!*

The funniest part of her telling this story, though, and the reason why we eventually began to goad her into it, was that she would demonstrate. She'd get this slack look on her face, push back her chair, bend right over so that her chin was almost touching her plate and shovel mashed potatoes into her mouth, just like the woman. To show us how ugly it looked, she said. If we weren't careful we'd end up that way, she said.

Again and again some elusive ballast in the telling of that story kept her coming back to it, kept us slipping in our table manners so she'd tell it one more time, so she'd take us one more time to the edge of the place where you aren't quite sure anymore who is who. Then we'd roll our eyes to quell the gap there and ask, each in our turn, to be excused.

᷂

We moved her to the same place she used to volunteer at. Played piano for the old folks every Sunday afternoon. The place just around the corner, block and a half away. I looked after her a long time, though, before we finally moved her to the Home. After all, I've got the nurse's training. By the end I had to do it all, and not just the cooking and cleaning. I took her to the bathroom, cleaned her up when she made a mess. Things a man shouldn't have to do for his wife. Though she always did love it when I'd wash her hair. Like they say, in sickness and in health.

Had to watch her like a hawk there at the end. She'd put the coffee on with no pot under it and the coffee'd go spurting all over the kitchen. She'd put the milk back in the cupboard under the sink beside the compost bucket and I'd come across it two days later, sour. I remember one day she came out of her bedroom in the morning wearing pantyhose with two bathing suits over them and a dress-shirt of mine over that. She was waving her arms down around her legs saying, *I don't like it so bare down here.* Funny what occurs to you at times like that. Dressing for all her different lives, I thought—pantyhose of a schoolteacher, bathing suits of a lady with a pool in her backyard where all the neighbourhood kids come to swim, borrowed dress shirt of a woman who's just plain confused.

I don't know quite why, but that day was the straw that broke my back. I recall steering her to the piano—she could still play with both hands then, and it was the only thing that gave me a break. I pulled out the stool, set the sheet music

in front of her, put her hands on the keys at middle C and
left her playing so I could rest my head in my hands in the
kitchen.

≈

I phoned her one Sunday
she phoned me the next

I phoned her one Sunday
she phoned me the next

༄

I volunteer once or twice a week at the Brant County Crisis Line. When I started Peter said, *Mary, you'll just never learn to say no, will you?* But they'd put a notice in the church bulletin saying they were in need of volunteers, and I thought I should give it a go. It's all confidential of course, I'm not even supposed to tell Peter, but what I *can* tell you is that there are an awful lot of lonely souls out there. Some of the other volunteers seem to be able to tell right away if a caller is high on drugs, but I must say I have a hard time telling the difference between the drug addicts and the callers who are just plain strange. I always take an egg salad sandwich or a ham and cheese, cut in quarters for a four-hour shift. It helps to pass the time. Some days hardly anyone calls at all.

In any case, plenty of the people who call the crisis line aren't really suicidal. Some of them are just simply in over their heads. Sometimes a single mother will call at her wits' end saying that she saw the crisis line number in the lineup at the food bank, and you can hear the baby crying in the background and you can tell from her grammar and her diction what kind of family she comes from, if you take my meaning. Sometimes I positively long to interrupt and say, *We were, dear, not we was.*

And some of the callers are just old. Those are the calls I do best with—I like to think of them as my specialty in a way, although it doesn't work that way of course. There's one old lady who calls every once in a while rather confused—can't remember when garbage day is and can't for the life of her figure out how to find out. Or sometimes she'll call us to find out what day of the week it is. Once she called while I was on shift and she was crying, saying, *I just dropped a vase full of freesia on the kitchen floor. What should I do?* she kept saying, *Help me Martha, I don't know what to do.* She sometimes calls us Martha, so that's what they've christened her in the logbook, Martha, though I pointed out in one of my logbook entries that her name isn't Martha—that's obviously the name of somebody else in her life, so it doesn't really fit to call *her* Martha, if you see what I mean. Well in any case, technically we're not supposed to encourage this kind of call, and some of the other volunteers have tried to make referrals—set her up with local homecare you know—but I don't mind talking to her when she calls. It's nice and satisfying to have some concrete way to be of help sometimes. I always picture her in a kitchen rather like my own, only with a crucifix where our clock is. She must be Catholic. *Lord have mercy, Lord have mercy,* she's always saying. *Lord have mercy,* between every sentence.

Of course, there are the times when we get a call from somebody who's actually suicidal. If there's somebody else on shift I'll pass it on to them. They try to always pair up a less experienced volunteer with one who has more experience. Once, though, Marie-Lou Cromwell, who's actually a therapist in real life, called in sick at the last moment and there was no one to replace her, so I was on shift all by myself. I usually take afternoon shifts since I'm retired, and from reading the logbook you get the idea that most of the suicide calls are night shift ones. In any case, this one day when I was all alone, wouldn't you know it, I got a real suicide call. I could tell right away it was serious because the young man's voice was so distant and his silences were so... well, so silent. And long. Oh I can still remember those silences. Gives me a shiver thinking of them. I was trying to juggle so many things at once—trying to remember everything I'd learned in the training about techniques for drawing a person out—what to say, what not to say, and at the same time trying not to remember how in the training my instinct was always to say the exact thing you're not supposed to say, and then trying to remember all the business about making a contract, getting the caller to make you a promise, and at the same time trying to find out where they are so you can send the police, and all the while trying to give them a sense that there's something to live for. Well, for pity's sake. All that and at the same time making sure they know you're really listening because they can tell, you know, and sometimes they'll just hang up on you if your mind is wandering. But then on the other hand trying not to be pushy or say too much because they'll hang up then, too. All that whirling around my head like a blizzard in those silences of his.

Well finally, after about four or five silences when I kept thinking he was completely gone and then I'd just manage to fish him back in, he was off again, and, well, I couldn't help myself; I just reached the end of my rope. I sat up straight and said, *Open your curtains.* Just like that. *What?* he said from far away. *Open your curtains. You're in the dark, aren't you?* I said. *How did you know?* he said, closer now. *Just a guess,* I said. *Now what do you say you go and open your curtains and let in a little light. It's a beautiful day out, and we're getting nowhere in the dark,* I told him, and he said, *I'm in a basement apartment, lady.* Just like that. *Well, for Pete's sake there still must be windows,* I said, and he said, *Yeah but they're all dirty.* Just like a child. *Well there's got to be a way to get some light in there,* I said, and he said, *I guess if I open the door to the outside it would give me some light.* And I said, *You go and do that now, but don't hang up. Come back and talk to me again as soon as you're done.* Okay, he said, and I'll tell you I held my breath the whole time he was gone. Finally he came back and picked up the phone and I let out my breath and I could hear him breathing too. After a while I said, *Hi.* *Hi,* he said, and he started to weep. *There, there,* I kept saying. *There, there.*

Well, in any case, apart from a few exceptions I'd say a good number of the callers are just plain lonely, and I don't mind chatting with them, or rather, letting them chat to me. I've occasionally even caught myself thinking wouldn't it be nice to have someone I could call—anonymously, you know— and never have to face the person and just be able to pour my heart out. Though I certainly don't let myself indulge that thought for very long. I'm not that sort of person and when you get right down to it, if you ask me, you take a risk letting yourself go like that—there's no telling whether you're going to be able to get yourself back. It's a slippery slope, as they say. Not that I blame the callers exactly. They're mostly all a little touched. But I do find myself impatient from time to time as a woman goes on and on about her problems and I get an urge to just interrupt, you know, just put an end to her nonsense. Tell her to just buck up. *Just dig deep dear,* I'd like to say. *You just need to decide. Your baby is crying, I can hear it. Stop talking about yourself, hang up the phone and go to your child. Just remember there's always somebody worse off than you are,* that's what I say. Or, at least, that's what I'd like to say, sometimes.

～

Lois King, UCW, on the tea-pouring incident

Once, before there was any kind of diagnosis, before even any kind of alarm—although who knows what she felt, she never said and, to be honest, it didn't occur to me to ask her until it was too late and she couldn't have said even if she'd wanted to, though I don't suppose she'd have said much, she never was one to complain—well anyway, she was pouring tea, looking right at the cup and spout, her one hand on the lid and, well, she just kept pouring. It was a UCW meeting, I seem to remember. She was chairing of course, but I don't believe she was talking. In fact, I don't think anyone was talking at the time. Or, if they were, they stopped as soon as the cup began to overflow. In fact, I seem to remember it felt like a chain reaction of sorts. The cup filling and beginning to brim, and the hush in the room rising in the same way. I remember thinking it looked lovely, actually, a kind of amber fountain, spilling over the edges of the cup into the saucer, then over the saucer into the tray, steaming. I remember thinking, if only the cup handle weren't there it would look so symmetrical. Now doesn't that just take the cake? You see, the curious thing was that we all just sat there watching her pour and pour until someone, I think it was Eleanor Davies, snapped out of it and said her name. *Mary.* I remember how gently Eleanor said it. And I remember she looked up and stopped pouring, both at the same time, as if her chin and the spout were attached by a string, like a marionette. Only not from above if you see what I mean.

Well. I admit it was awkward then for a moment. As if a spell were broken or a dish or—oh something awkward, I don't know. Eleanor got up, helped her put the teapot down and led her by the elbow through the kitchen into the front room. The rest of us still sitting there. Of course it didn't take long for someone to break the silence, change the subject you know, and then we all gradually started to chat again. I remember we talked about that new bylaw, the one that says cats ought to be put on leashes of all things. None of us referred to the incident, except, when I slipped out to the kitchen with the tray to clean it up a bit, Margaret George followed. She touched me on my forearm with those everlasting cold hands of hers and asked me in a whisper what did I make of it. I didn't have time to answer though, because just then Eleanor and Mary came back in and everything went on as usual. Mind you, I could tell everyone was a little shaken. When you get to be our age, it's all a little too close to home.

≈

Honest to goodness I never saw anything to beat it. That woman would push her plate out in front of her—just like this—and hunker down—look I'll show you. Like this. On her elbows! Not a word of a lie! And then she'd shovel the food into her mouth, not lifting at all. Look. And she held the fork like this—for all the world like an oar! Just like this, not even lifting her arm one bit. Not a word of a lie. Well. I couldn't eat at the same table with her. Had to take my meal afterward standing at the sideboard in the kitchen. Now let that be a lesson to you. Honest to goodness.

&

things that still have not left her

1 chewing
with her mouth closed

2 disdain
for the strength of my grandfather's
coffee

3 the ability to sound out words
from whatever's on the coffee table—articles on
bear attacks in *Reader's Digest,*
sexual assaults in the local paper,
the sanctuary roof leaking in the church bulletin—
each word falling apart behind her the moment
she moves onto the next

4 the ability to return a compliment
for example: when Uncle Nick says,
What a nice dress you have on Mom
she says in return, *And yours is nice too*

5 sight-reading the melody line from sheet music
when put in front of a piano, she can still
play the right
hand

6 smiling
when kissed

~

The kiss James gave me on his way out to give a guitar lesson this morning was different somehow. A hint of a stranger. I wanted badly to know what gave it this flavour of newness. A certain restraint? A new tongue technique? Something in his bearing said, *I could surprise you.* His hand, on its way to my back, brushed my breast only glancingly, almost as if by accident, as if there were lines we hadn't yet crossed together. His other hand holding his guitar case. Something in the way he kept a slight distance made me feel unexplored—curious and worthy of curiosity.

To hold back. Not say. Leave untouched. Camp out nearby. Admire from a distance. Go to the edge but not enter. Heidegger's pilgrimage to the Greek island of Delos: when he finally got there he found he'd imagined the sacred site so clearly and so often and the sight of it from the boat so matched and even surpassed his imaginings, that he couldn't bring himself to disembark.

To not get off the ferry. To not set foot on shore. To stay at sea.

We need more kisses like that one.

※

Lois King, on the chrysanthemums

I think for a long time none of us admitted even to ourselves what was happening. Then there came a point you couldn't deny it anymore. It was in the spring when it dawned on me. Or the summer. When do mums bloom? She brought chrysanthemums that day. From their garden, of course. Peter always had such a lovely garden. I passed by there the other day, by their old place on Silver Street. Such a shame it's all gone to seed now. Any-hoo, I remember it was a UCW meeting and I was hosting—it was my turn. Peter must have dropped her off, but she didn't even knock. I just happened to open the door because I'd burnt the orange loaf and I wanted to let in a little fresh air. Lord knows how long she'd been standing there with that big bunch of yellow chrysanthemums in her arms, the ends all wrapped in damp paper towels. I could tell right away by the look on her face when I opened the door and saw her standing on the front stoop with an armful of mums, her forehead tight and her eyes on the doorbell, well, I could tell that she was having one of her bad days. That's what we'd been calling it, she and I, *her bad days.* So before taking her inside I just stepped out onto the porch with her and took the flowers and gave her a little hug with one arm and whispered in her ear, *Just try to keep a stiff upper lip, Mary—it'll be fine, just fine.* I don't know how I knew what to say. Normally I'm plain useless in those kinds of situations. I clam right up. But somehow the words just came to me. She looked at me with a kind of—relief.

A kind of devoted relief, and we went inside, arm in arm. I remember thinking it was the kind of look you get from a hurt child or a dog or a man who's just fallen in love with you. That was when I knew she was never going to be the same. She sort of stuck nearby me that day and didn't say much, but when she did it wasn't anything out of order. I remember when Peter came to pick her up, I made a point of praising his chrysanthemums.

≈

Peter Peter pumpkin
eater Mary Mary quite
contrary had a wife and

               how
does your garden grow?

~~

When Mary was still home, she'd soak her teeth in a water glass overnight. Had all her real teeth pulled years ago—dentist in Brantford said it'd be easier in the long run. On nights I couldn't sleep, I used to look at her beside me sometimes. Sleeping away there. Toothless. Face sunken like a landslide. Whole landscape changed. Middle-of-the-night thoughts, you know.

Lost her teeth at the nursing home last week. Nurse on duty just shrugged her skinny shoulders and told me, *You keep valuables here at your own risk.* Bitches, all of 'em. Want to know how much I pay every month to the goddamn crooks who own the place? Orientals now. Well, let's just say it put me in a state. Worst part of it was nobody willing to give me a bloody straight answer as to what I should do. Had me walking around all week debating this way and that whether or not to replace the things. Costs hundreds to replace a whole set of dentures. Hundreds. I called Ruth long distance and she wasn't any help. Ran into Lois King in the grocery store on Thursday, and she wouldn't say a thing either, not even when I asked straight out, *Do you think she even knows the goddamn difference?* All of them just shrugging their shoulders. *It's up to you, Dad. Whatever you think is best, Peter.* By the end of the week, I caught myself talking right out loud about it as I was digging up the glads. *Christ,* I said to myself, *all the food in the place is mush anyhow—the bastards are afraid of being sued for choking—what does she need teeth for?* But then I'd walk the block and a half to visit her and her face was a different face, not hers, not her own you know—more like a goddamn natural disaster than a face—and I'd end up going home early so I wouldn't have to look at her anymore.

Then this morning I woke up even earlier than usual. Hours until the light. I was staring at the whatsisname. Group of Seven man. Lawren Harris. The Lawren Harris picture in the bedroom. The one of the iceberg or whatever the hell it is. The one I never liked. Always thought it was too cold, but she had a soft spot for it. All I can say is, staring at that painting, something came clear in me. Just like that. It was like I'd been looking at a small part of the thing, and now all of a sudden I saw the whole of it. I don't know. All I can say is the hours I had to wait then until the dentist's office opened at nine o'clock and the receptionist finally answered the phone, well, I'd be lying if I didn't say they were some of the longest hours I've lived.

❧

Peter read somewhere the other day that you've got to be careful about the sugar water in your hummingbird feeder —it can ferment in the sun if you leave it too long, and then you've got a crew of drunken hummingbirds on your hands. Fancy that. I suppose you could even kill them. Now wouldn't that be a crying shame? A crying shame. Peter was reading an article in his gardening magazine the other day, and do you know what? They say that if you leave the sugar water in your hummingbird feeder too long it will ferment. Into alcohol. Think of it. You'd have a crew of drunken hummingbirds on your hands. A crying shame.

~

When Mom told me on the phone about them losing Grandma's teeth at the nursing home I remembered that someone once told me if you dream of your teeth falling out, it means you're feeling out of control.

When I said that to Mom, she hung up on me. Actually hung up on me.

It was bizarre, but I have to admit, for some reason I felt sort of proud of her.

❧

I phoned her one Sunday
She phoned me the next

I phoned her one Sunday

Then   I don't know when
I just phoned every Sunday

For the life of me
I don't know when

the song of the
red-breasted,
white-throated
auctioneer

.

&

HEYANDwho'llgimme50forthewashboardhere
who'llgimmeandgo50andgo50Ihave50doIhear52
dollarabiddollarabiddollarabidnow52Ihear52
doIhear55,55who'llgimme55Ihave55,60overhere
HEYwillyabiddollarabiddollarabid60doIhear65
who'llgimme65forthewashboardfolksnicewashboard
makemusicwithyourlaundryfolks65,65doIhear65,62
okay62Ihave62overinthecorner here once twice

65Ihave65hey'llyabiddollarabiddollarabidwhat'llya
bid65 once twice ma'am?no? once twice
                                    SOLD
to the lady with her husband's hand over her mouth

ঐ

Dear Mr. Phipps,

Your letter was not addressed to me, it was addressed to my wife who I am sorry to say is afflicted with Alzheimer's disease, which I am sure you probably have heard of. She's gotten to be so far gone she is not able to manage our letters and affairs anymore, so that is why I opened your letter that was addressed to her and read it. I am sure you won't mind.

My wife must have gotten her name on many a list over the last few years so that I am almost every day opening letters that are asking her for money, and I have just about reached my limit. I have taken to pitching most all of them now, although that can be a tricky business too because if you don't open them you never know if maybe it was a bill or some such important thing like that. I am writing to tell you that I will not be sending any more money because as I said I have reached my limit and have moved my wife to the Home, and that costs a pretty penny and leaves not too much left over. However one idea occurred to me the other day as I was turning the compost heap, a heavy job. I have always been a strong man but my body is not what it used to be as I am now eighty-seven years of age and I am finding it hard to keep up with the work around the place this spring, especially the garden. I was thinking about all the letters and about why should I be giving money to help all these other folks when I was giving all my life, a regular churchgoer and always ready to lend a hand, and now here I am in need of a bit of help these days myself. Not that I want to go around feeling sorry for myself, but all the same. Then I was recalling one of the letters had something to say about orphans and right then and there I dropped the shovel and went inside and went rooting around in the wastebasket until I found that letter and sure enough it turned out to be from yourself at the Covenant House, a home for runaways and homeless youths, as it states in your letter.

I guess you can see what I'm about here. It seems to me Mr. Phipps to make good sense instead of sending money I can't spare that I help by offering room and board to one of your young lads in exchange for some help around this place on his part. Even when my wife was able to cook I used to take a turn in the kitchen now and then, and being a male nurse after I sold the farm I have the nurse's training which includes a course on nutrition and all the women nurses were amazed at how I could make muffins from scratch, so I am a good cook and I could offer a small weekly sum of money, which I don't think he would find objectionable. It may not be precisely what a young man has in mind to live with an old man like myself and I am the first to admit I can be stubborn sometimes, but on the whole I don't think it would be all bad and as I said I have plenty of work to be done around here and it's always good for a man to work hard when he is young and in his prime, so I could probably teach him a thing or two and I expect we could get along tolerably well, two bachelors. Perhaps you should choose a quiet one, as I live a quiet life, especially now that my wife Mary Friesen is in the Home. When I owned the farm I used to get hired men every spring from the government employment office and they always were sending me the foreign ones as I speak German, Ukrainian,

Russian and I can get by in Dutch as it is so similar to the Low German dialect of my Mennonite forefathers. So I am familiar with being a good boss, I was always fair, all the pickers always wanted to work the Friesen farm come harvest.

So if you will stop sending me your letters and send me instead one of your boys I would be much obliged. Please write soon as it would be nice to get the boy in time to help with the summer yard and garden work.

Thanking you, I am yours truly,

Peter Friesen

~

Grandpa fell up the stairs in July and down the stairs in August.

For several springs now he must have planted the sugar snap peas with the awareness that it could be the last time. He loves to get the timing right. Outwit the frosts. Get the buggers in there so they're high as his hip by early June, high as his shoulder by late June and bearing six-quart baskets every other day by the first week in July. He used to give baskets of peas to the nurses at the hospital. Now he gives them to the staff at the nursing home. He still gives them to the ladies who come to swim three times a week even though Grandma isn't there anymore. *Eat 'em raw,* he says, *sure! Sugarsnaps. They're sugarsnap peas not snow peas. Sugarsnap. Go ahead. Try one.*

He orders the seeds early. I imagine he and Grandma used to sit down together with the seed catalogue on an afternoon in February, the sun coming in the back window, both of them with an utter and unconsidered faith in the coming of spring.

So for a while now he's probably planted knowing it could be the last time. I imagine this brings the focus up sharp— each pea poked into its hole with his thick forefinger, the meticulous stringing of the trellis, the knots harder to fashion each year.

This spring too. Each pea, each knot, sharp, noticed. But maybe this year there's also a new feeling—a heaviness, a background worry. Let's say by the second day of planting he's conscious of it and is trying to put his finger on the feeling. By afternoon he has it: at the same time that he's worried this will be the last time, he's also worried it *won't* be the last time.

He's always pictured himself dying on his own two feet—keeling over in his garden, falling back into the raspberry bushes with a hat on his head and a hoe in his hand. He's always assumed that's how it would be. Ever since the heart attack ten years ago. He's been almost proud of it, as if the heart attack was a pure expression of his personality. Now, suddenly, he's afraid he won't manage it. That he'll end up in the Home like the others. Not for me, he's always told himself. Now it strikes him for the first time that it's not for him to decide.

He leaves the hoe and packet of radish seeds in the middle of the row and walks to the back door of the house, takes off his hat and steps inside to lie down. It is the first time in his life he's laid down indoors in the middle of the afternoon for no good reason.

The next day he's up early, making himself a big bowl of cream of wheat. He dresses himself, whistling all the while, in his thick coveralls and work gloves and the heavy canvas jacket from Massey Ferguson. He walks out into the garden, walks right by the seed packet and hoe all wet with dew, and on into the raspberry patch. It's a big patch, and recently it's gotten so he hasn't been able to keep up with the pruning. Damn canes haven't been bearing worth beans last few years. A red-winged blackbird watches from the fence post. Used to be so as you couldn't keep up with them, but last summer you'd have been lucky to fill the bottom of a pie plate. Should have cleared the things out last fall. Too damn sentimental. Well, their time's come.

He sets to work. First with the scythe but then with whatever he can put his hands on to do the job. The saw. The shovel. The axe in a couple of places. By noon he's got the patch pretty well loosened up and is going at it mostly with his hands. *Thorny bastards.* Right through his gloves in a couple of places. And into his wrists all along the gap between his glove-ends and his jacket cuffs. He bleeds easily these days because of the heart pills. Doesn't care. He's breathing hard, sweating, his heart thumping so violently at one point he thinks it must be disturbing the rest of his insides. He stops every now and then to listen to his hoof-beat heart, but not long. Not too long. He keeps working, wrestling the raspberry canes. He stops at two for some warmed-up soup and toast. Then back at it. By twilight the raspberry patch is in irreparable disarray and he is tired, tired, so tired he's close to weeping. He goes to bed that night without supper and with his coveralls on. The next day he calls Lois King and asks her to send her grandson over to finish the job. The grandson lives in town. High school student. Good kid. He doesn't call Ruthie or Nick.

It takes him over a week to recover, and even then he doesn't fully. Not quite. Not ever. He trembles, can't will his legs sometimes to stand him up and walk him to the kitchen, so he sits in his chair just thinking about tea, just thinking. That summer there is only a half a row of radishes and no one notices.

In July he falls on his way up the stairs of the front porch to get the mail. He never uses the front door, always in and out by the side door near the back. Every couple of days he walks around the house up onto the front porch and fetches the mail from the mailbox. He trips and falls face-first, skins his knees and chin. He turns over, sits up and then sits there on the front porch, sobbing, his knees bleeding through his pants.

He falls again in August. Down the stairs this time, the stairs to the basement. He's carrying a jar of freshly pickled plum tomatoes, and all he can think as he's falling is, *I can't let the jar break.* He falls to the bottom. Nothing is broken, neither the jar nor his bones, but he is badly bruised and can barely breathe. He doesn't call anyone to tell them about the fall. Ruth shows up on the weekend to visit, sees the bruises, hears the story. When she goes downstairs to use the basement bathroom, she notices the jar of pickled tomatoes off to the side on the floor at the foot of the stairs, like a stone marking a grave or a well.

That autumn he gives in and decides to sell the house, his last crop of sugar snap peas already planted and harvested.

꙰

Johnny Schritt had a scow he used for fishing so when the Red River flooded that year he figured he was king of the mountain for a while, and a generous king at that. It was my first season as a hired man on Henry Lytle's farm but Johnny had been there for years. When the floods came he took us all for rides in his scow and didn't even charge us, grateful, I suppose, to be centre of attention for once cause no one (least of all women) had ever looked twice at Johnny Schritt, at least not since he was born with his toes attached like that to one another. He was the sort of fellow who couldn't follow a set of instructions to save his hide but who knew every type of useless trick you could think of. Like how to cheat at racehorse rummy or how to put a chicken to sleep by tucking her head under her wing and swinging her back and forth between your legs like a pendulum for a minute or two. Johnny would be on his way to feed the pigs and out of the blue he'd grab a chicken from the yard and put her to sleep like that, then climb up to the loft in the barn and set the chicken on the rafter beam so that when she woke up a minute later she'd find herself way up high there in the air. Jesus you should have heard the sounds those chickens made then.

Anyhow, a whole lot of neighbours were camping out with us—the Lytle place was one of the farms on high ground there. Johnny and I gave up our beds in the bunkhouse for the women and kids, and the men all slept in the barn. All the farmers were worried sick about when the rain would stop, the waters go down, land dry up enough for spring planting. They'd be up half the night figuring—you could hear them making figures together about the cost of buying new seed and how late they could push it and still get in a harvest before frost. And even when they weren't talking it over, it was on their minds. Round the clock. You could see it in their faces if you caught sight of one of them looking out over the fields of water—you could tell they were chewing it over inside their heads, figuring. You could almost hear them grinding their teeth, willing the water to disappear, wishing for a Moses to part it, or a Jesus to tame it, or wishing at the very least that a Noah had saved their livestock two by two.

Johnny and I slept up in the hayloft and let them talk. Johnny was a little thick and didn't give two hoots for anything but excitement, and to me nothing could be as bad as what I'd seen in the Old Country. Seemed to me hunger and blood were different when there was looting and bayonets to blame—unnatural you might say. So flood or no flood, this was the land of plenty to me and I wasn't going to waste time worrying.

In the days after the rain finally stopped but before the water started back to where it belonged, Johnny ran himself ragged taking us all for excursions in his leaky little scow. He and I went on our own the first trip. Had to take turns rowing and bailing. Took us a while to get there at first. We tried to follow the road to town but kept getting either lost or beached, so after a spell I talked Johnny into giving the current a go and we followed the river. Didn't have to row at all, all the way to town, just lean back and drift. I remember putting my hands up on either side of my face like horse blinkers, turning around until at one particular angle I got a glimpse of pure water almost as far as you could see, flat as a field of wheat only silver instead of gold and I tell you I was in my glory.

Sure was a funny feeling floating over the town bridge instead of under. The water was murky as hell, but I can still remember to this day looking down over the edge of Johnny Schritt's scow that first trip into town after the rain stopped and seeing a row of automobiles like great big stones just under the surface of the water, parked all along Main Street as if nothing at all was amiss, just minding their own business. The dogwood had already turned red in front of the credit union and you could just barely make it out as you passed over, a red blur, waving like in the wind. 'Course downtown there were plenty of tall two-storey brick buildings so it was no problem to get your bearings there. On the way home it was hard going—upstream, you know. You had to take care not to get disoriented 'cause in some places for long stretches there were only rooftops showing by the river and one rooftop tends to look a hell of a lot like another whether you're rich or poor.

Johnny and I were tight friends so he took me on almost every excursion as first mate to his skipper. Wasn't so much fun after that first trip though. The water started to go down quickly so it wasn't as grand and we got beached more and more often and everyone was worrying over their houses, wanting to go visit their property, figure the damage. At the time I remember being impatient and all full of scorn, but looking back, who can blame them?

I never forgot that time. I slept at night in the Lytles' barn with my arms and back aching from rowing upstream and my dreams all fast and blurred and turned around. When I went to sleep I'd be caught right up in a current again, right where it left off. I remember the dreams went on for a spell even after the water was gone. They were full of things showing up in places they shouldn't be. The milking bucket turning up in Mrs. Lytle's china cabinet. The pipe organ from the church standing in the back pasture among the cattle. My sister Anne in the bow of the boat leaning back like Cleopatra even though she'd already gone east by then. And in one dream the pine box we made to bury Father—it was perched on the beams of the Lytle barn for all the world like one of Johnny Schritt's sleeping chickens.

~

This morning two workmen come to fix the plumbing in the apartment downstairs. One of them knocks on my door, wants to come up and turn on the water. I let him up, but I'm instantly aware that his nose won't be adjusted to the stink of out-of-control sauerkraut in the pantry where the sink is. So I go in and turn on the tap for him. He listens, says thanks, goes back downstairs. Of course when he leaves I'm finally motivated to deal with the stink, though James has been bugging me to deal with it for days. So I'm kneeling on the floor scooping scum off the sauerkraut with a teaspoon into a blue plastic cup, and through the floorboards I hear the one workman telling the other how my place stinks, how disgusting it is, how there's definitely something rotting up there. *Hurry up so we can get out of here*, the other one says.

So I start pacing and, even though I half-know they'll be gone before I get to them, I'm working up my courage to go down, knock on the door and explain that I heard them through the floorboards, up through the pipes—explain about the sauerkraut, how I hate the stink too, how I wish I could just dump the whole fucking crock into the compost except I don't have a compost so it would have to be the garbage, but that I can't, because, you see, because of my grandfather.

Because—how to explain—because of the small messages he leaves to himself on scraps of paper all over his house (*veterinarian appointment Tues 1 pm, that cat will be the death of me*), and because of the shaky hand he writes them in.

Because his house is for sale and I'm guessing this was the

last time we'll ever make sauerkraut together. Because his old cat Tigger died the day before I went over there to make the sauerkraut. Because Tigger is buried with an upside-down washbasin to mark his grave under the apple tree that Grandpa tried to splice with pear.

Because the man poured pickle juice on his fried rice when we ordered Chinese after making the sauerkraut. Because I tried it too. And it was good.

Because the first year I made sauerkraut with him I told everyone, *Did you know there's no vinegar in sauerkraut—only cabbage and salt, fermented.* Because no one knew. It was always news.

Because we have the same taste for vinegar. Because I don't speak Low German or German or Ukrainian or Russian or Dutch.

Because the lantern that used to light his way to the barn for morning chores now hangs unlit in my living room.

Because he bought thirty cabbages and bragged to the Mennonite woman who sold them that his granddaughter wanted to learn sauerkraut.

Because she was impressed.

Because he wouldn't tell me when I'd stomped enough juices out of the cabbage with the wooden cudgel. I had to guess for myself. Because he used to have Polish farmhands who made huge wooden kegs of sauerkraut. Because they'd walk on it in their bare feet. Like Mediterraneans walk on grapes. For wine.

And I'm crying now because I'm such a sad sorry sap and I'm about to get my period and I'm behind on my rent and I'm back in the pantry kneeling in front of the sauerkraut scooping the scum into a blue plastic cup holding my breath in the stink and my nose is running and I'm wiping it on my sleeve and trying not to sob too loudly as the plumbers gather up their tools below.

～

things buried with us

1
The clicking sound
her knees made
whenever she bent
or straightened.

2
One Saturday afternoon
in front of the general store
a starling swooped close,
and she was not startled.

3
When pregnant with her first child, she had
a womb-name for it which she never told anyone
(though once quite near her
time she wrote it down in pencil
on the back of a recipe card
as she waited
for her pie to set).

4
He bought an old violin once because he had
a certain idea of himself. It buckles
slowly, stringless
in its black-lacquered case in my closet.

5

Long ago a secret formed
a lump in his throat that gradually
became part of his profile. She also

had a secret—who knows
if it was the same as his or
different or somehow
both. Whatever the case, over the years
it was incorporated into how she held her face
so when you see her in her coffin you will barely
recognize her—forehead, cheeks and jaw
unclenched; face slack, loose, almost
universal; the secret
gone before her into the earth.

6

There was a certain teacup, a tallish lily of the valley cup, its
silhouette like a fleshy neck smoothed out by the chin held high.

It was the one she was drinking from when the hospital phoned
with the news of her father's death.

She placed the cup at the back of the buffet, behind the gravy
boat, Christmas platter and crystal pickle tray.

Years later, when the house was sold, the contents auctioned
off, the buffet and china cabinet cleared out, the auctioneer's
assistant picked up the cup,
                                        wondered ever-so-briefly why
it was separate,
then put it together
with the rest.

7

Almost everything
is buried with us:
once she ate a shallow bowl full of wild
strawberries that took her the better part
of the morning to pick.
She was eating them all
by herself
with a spoon on the side stoop and,
looking up at the oak in the yard,
said aloud, *Fancy*
meeting you
here.

❧

High Park, a walk on my way to work.

Leaves at their absolute peak, sunlight pouring profligate from bluest sky. Luminous oranges, rusts and yellows on all sides as I walk, scuba diver among vibrant reefs.

In the off-leash area of the park somebody's whippet has a squirrel in its jaws. The squirrel, still alive, clawing at the dog's cheeks. The dog's tail wagging.

What kind of world is this?

Lately the smallest thing—one firm section of an orange, say, with its thin translucent skin and, when you break it open, its grain of crowded nodules, each slim nodule a pocket of juice contained within an even thinner skin, all of it bright orange but somehow pale at the same time, variable, as if an emissary of the sun itself, not to mention the white pith just bitter enough to make the sweetness sing—the smallest thing

can hold me firmly, perfectly in place for a whole afternoon, like a paperweight.

That we are here at all (even the words *we* and *here*—even

words) seems fantastical. On my way to work, to bathe old people like babies. Washcloth between their toes, luxury of warm water over their backs. They stare at me, amazed that these wrinkled folds—these bent, knobby, unreliable limbs—are their very own.

There is nothing that is not exotic.

We're all, all of us, just visiting.

$\hat{\sigma}$

The youngster who finally buys the house offers a figure way under the listing price—under even Grandpa's bottom line—and won't negotiate about buying the appliances. It's the first offer he's had for six weeks but Grandpa, stubborn and insulted, refuses to counter-offer. The real estate agent calls Mom and Uncle Nick, and they intervene.

There are four lists:
> things to be moved to Grandpa's new apartment
> things to be taken by family
> things to be auctioned off
> things to be sold privately

(And the items that don't make any of the lists. An anti-list: things to be loaded into the back of the auctioneer's pickup truck for the dump.)

～

When I get there the weekend before the auction, he's in the driveway with the red wagon behind him—full of houseplants to take to his new apartment in the seniors' building attached to the nursing home a block and a half away. It's one of those crisp, late fall mornings, and we can see our breath as we hug.

Mom said the auctioneer came during the week to box and categorize but I can't really tell the difference; his workshop is still a colossal clutter: boxes of soil-caked teacup saucers mixed with wrenches and screwdrivers, stacks of six-quart baskets stuffed with steel wool and seed packets. In a copper boiler, coils of garden hose. I point out the boiler to Grandpa. "You might as well take it," he says. "It'll just go in the auction for two bits."

Lifting out the hoses, Grandpa says he once met a Baptist who had a theory—said he'd figured out the reason why ropes and hoses and necklaces inevitably tangle even if they're left coiled neatly. *It's because of the Fall,* he said.

All fall Uncle Nick has been taking home carpentry tools, Grandpa has been salvaging what he'll need in his small apartment, I've been picking things out for my apartment. I'd pick something up, and Grandpa would look at it, snort. "What're you taking that old thing for?"

Even before this all started, before he announced he was selling the house, even then the workshop already looked plundered—not plundered by a son's hobby or a granddaughter's fancy or an auctioneer's weary categories, but by the disorder that rises as naturally as weeds or cream when you leave anything be: the hummingbird feeder stuck upside down in an old tobacco tin; a cracked outdoor thermometer, mercury gone; a yellowing page—hand-drawn pictures of tools—torn from Eaton's catalogues and tacked up. When you pulled at random from the set of little drawers meant for nuts and bolts and nails, sometimes you'd find those things—nuts and bolts and nails—sometimes a nest of old filigreed keys, a greasy tangle of string, shoe tacks in with a flat tin of lozenges.

Beside that, an empty drawer. Beside that, birdseed and hinges.

Below that, a ball bearing and a slip of paper with some words written in a different alphabet.

Just before I have to leave, as he and I are sitting in silence at the table with empty teacups, he starts to sing in Russian, maybe Ukrainian. When he's finished we sit there for a long time.

It seems incredibly important somehow, but I can't remember now whether I asked him to translate or whether he just did:

> Oh Uncle tell me
> is this life all for nothing
> Moscow is burning
> and the French are all around

꩜

Contents of the shed everbodyhadachancetotakea
lookattheshed?welltoughifyadidn'twe'restartinthe
biddin HEYwillyabid20doIhear20 25overhere30
Ihear30dollarabiddollarabiddoIhave35 35for
everythingintheshedIhear40 40 45overherefor45
hey'llyabidwho'llyabid 60! Ihave60 70 70 the shed
is hothotmustbesometreasureintheshedwho'llgimme
75 Ihave75 80 Ihave80dollarswhat'llyabiddollarabid
dollarabidwhat'llyabidnow Ihave80anyoneanyone
dollarabid85 Ihave85 88 88doIhear90 Ihave90 92
92overhere 94 94 sir?100? yessirhey'llyabid
dollarabidwouldyabidnow 100Ihaveonehundrednow
who'llgimme110 toorichforya?100

100

100

SOLD to number 21 in the back

(got that Mary-Anne?)

∂⌢

1

I stand there weighing one of Grandpa's old hand planes in my hands, pass my finger over the polished wooden knob on the front, leave behind a line in the dust. That certain kind of dust. Fine and thick and democratic. The kind you only find in old workshops and basements with a particular sort of foundation. The dust of authenticity and neglect.

The dilemma: do I keep the plane because it is beautiful, because it is my grandfather's, or do I give it to my downstairs neighbour, the woodworker, who says he can always use old tools, although, to be truthful, it's probably sentimentality on his part too; the new planes with plugs and motors and switches and who-knows-what do a much better job, and so much quicker it's ridiculous. I put the plane in a box and decide to decide later. In the end, when I get home and my neighbour's there, on a whim with a wake of regret, I hand it to him and go to bed without washing my hands.

2

I admit, holding the hand plane I considered learning the art of building furniture—doing it the way it once was done. I considered making it all by hand, only hand tools; I considered making that effort. I even asked myself, almost seriously, *What precisely makes it old? Where exactly do you draw the line?* I cut my finger testing the blade, drew blood and thought, *You need metal (the iron age was long ago)*. But how far to go back? No electricity? Or arbitrary: only tools made, say, before Grandpa sold his tobacco farm in 1961? How do you decide? And how do you explain yourself to those who do it quicker and better with new tools that aren't even really that expensive at Canadian Tire?

You don't.

The old art no longer makes sense in this element; it breathes another kind of air, wholly other lungs; it needs life support.

3

But what if you were to preserve the old art because the millennium has turned, and a part of you holds a belief—as firmly as your hand holds the polished hardwood knob on the front of the old plane—a belief that this civilization will someday collapse. There'll be no electricity. We'll need the old arts.

Could it be a practical act?

It's not even a belief, really—more
like a vision.
Of a burning city.
Of burning cities throughout
history. The Fall
of Rome. The Retreat
from Moscow. Troy. A sense
that our city is not immune. A certainty, a
lump in the throat as you walk home passing the East Indian

greengrocer, the hardware store, the wig shop that's been having a going-out-of-business sale for over three years, and the second-hand clothing store where the woman has an accent you can't place

and circles under her eyes
that you can.

~

The day of the auction people are already swarming the house when I arrive. They're everywhere—in the front room, the living room, the bedrooms, the kitchen, the basement, the yard, the shed. There's a guy all set up selling hot dogs in the workshop. I wander among them, anonymous, aware of the resistance of the screen door spring, of my hand on the railing on the way down to the basement, the too-steep stairs—all familiar, all mine, but no way to assert it, my allegiances so simple, so quiet, so accurate, so inconsequential.

The auctioneer calls out, *Watch that step folks, the last one's a lu-lu.*

In the end a small crock with the word *Berlin* on the bottom of it goes for $195. The brand new gas stove sells for $35 to the young man who bought the house.

"I'm about ready to sell my soul," says Grandpa.

꒱

Stan Felder, auctioneer

A man likes to have a job he's good at. Simple as that. Being an auctioneer is a calling I always say. Pun intended, of course. The way I see it is you're there to make it a good time. Amuse the crowd, so to speak. People like to let go. Be swept up, if you know what I'm saying. That's my job and as I said, I'm good at it. You see you gotta get the crowd going to your rhythm. Box them in and let them loose at the same time. Get 'em all caught up. Wave your arms around and get yourself right up into their faces some of the time. You gotta corner them with the patter and then, when you're sure you got them really going, once in a while—WHAM—outa nowhere, give 'em silence. Just like that. Silence. Then, calm as could be, *Would you bid forty?* Silence. Look her right in the eye. *Would you bid forty?* And she's got to say yes, she's got no choice but to nod and then you're off to the races again before they can even take in what happened. Yessir. You don't have to be particular with it all, just as long as they know the general range you're in doesn't matter one bit if you're at thirty-two or thirty-four dollars, you just keep sending the numbers up and around till they get the feeling like they gotta keep up. Just give them the gist is what I say to Norm. Cut off the word as soon as they got the idea and onto the next one, run 'em together fast as you can think—and we human beings we can think pretty goddamn fast, let me tell you. Faster than we think we can think. So it's not about punctuality. You don't have to be so particular is what I always say to

Norm, my nephew. Norm's trying to learn the patter. He helps me out at a weekend sale every now and then, holding things up for the crowd to see. Likes to picture himself up on the stool with the cane and all eyes on him, but I keep telling him it's a calling. *Norm, I say, you gotta stop being so goddamn serious about it*, pardon my French. You gotta have humour. Gotta amuse the crowd. That's the name of the game. Gotta make the people laugh. Let down their guard. Have a good time. That's why I always get Bob Cartwright to set up a concession someplace on the property—in the garage if there is one, or the barn, or out on the lawn if it's a fine day. Pop and foot-longs. Bob always gets onions frying on the grill. Gives people a good feeling to smell that. Makes them feel at home. The regulars always say something if Bob isn't there with his coffee urn and grill. He's one of them Kingdom Hall folks. But a good man—never tries to talk a fellow into any religion and I respect that. Well anyway the bottom line is you've got to have a way with people. You might say I'm a sort of a leader in the community. Not in the way of a doctor or mayor or minister, but a leader all the same. People tend to get the idea in their heads that auctions are the end of the road if you know what I mean. Death or bankruptcy or what have you, but I always say it doesn't have to be that way. No sir. An auction is like a party as far as I'm concerned, only better. It's party, commerce, community meeting and what they call these days a recycling effort—all rolled into one. Now what more could you ask for on a Saturday afternoon, I ask you that. Course there's the business side of things too. It's always in the back of my head so to speak that I want to get the best sum I can for the seller as much as I want to get it for my own commission, so it's not just greedy when I say I know how to work a crowd, by God. Yessirree. It's a public service as far as I'm concerned. In more ways than one. And it's a grand old time like I said. No, an auction doesn't have to be all doom and gloom like some folks would have you believe. Take for instance the one we held last Saturday just on the outskirts of the town of Paris. An old fellow selling off his place cause he can't take care of it properly anymore, you know the story. The daughter arranged it all with me and said she was going to stay away, didn't want any part of it. Fair enough I said to her, probably wise. The man himself only came for the end. I don't generally recommend it that the owners be present. Too many memories. But as it turned out the granddaughter was there the whole time, hanging about. A grown girl. Norm whispers in my ear at the break that she's wandering around, staring. Norm says he saw her asking some poor fellow if she could buy back something he'd already bought, telling him how she remembered it from when she was a kid. Making everybody feel a little antsy, if you know what I mean. So I come up to her and introduce myself. *You're the granddaughter, aren't you?* I say, *I heard you were around. You're the spitting image of your mother. I'm Stan Felder.* *Stan?* she says, her eyes wandering over my shoulder. *That's my name and you can go on ahead and wear it out all you like,* I say, and she smiles. *You got a nice property here. Lotsa memories,* I say, and her eyes start to tear up you know. So I lean in close and tap her on the nose with the handle of the cane and say, *Don't worry honey—it's got to be done and it's the best way to do 'er. Just relax and enjoy the show.* And she finally looks me in the eye and shakes my hand when I offer it and after that she wasn't so bad. Even bought herself a hot dog. You got to have a way with people. Yessiree. Like I said, it's a calling. Pun intended, of course.

∾

Too damn many sides to the story all the time. Makes me tired. Makes me just want to lie down. Bone-tired, like the saying is. I'm bone-tired these days. Air's cold if you go out but in this place it doesn't matter a bit what season it is outdoors—it's always too goddamn hot in here. Nick came and rigged up a fan on the bedroom ceiling where the light fixture is, so it goes on when you switch on the light. It's slow enough I can pick out one arm of the thing and follow it around and around and around. Makes me seasick though, so I keep one foot on the floor. One foot warm in the bed, one foot cold on the floor.

After a while I can't look at the fan anymore so I just turn my head to the side and look past the geraniums out the window. You'd be surprised how much of an afternoon a man can piss away lying on his bed staring out the window, not even at anything, just bare branches and sky.

That Lois King came around the other day, fussing. I'm guessing Ruth asked her to come and check up on me. She thinks I don't notice her going through my refrigerator throwing things out. Well this time I told her. Gave her a shock. Came up behind her and yes sir I told her. *Nothing's bad in there, it's all good,* I said. *Get your meddling hands out of my goddamn food.* They've all got it in their heads that you can't save a thing more than twenty-four hours. Got it in their heads I don't know what I'm about. Well it put her in a flap, that's for sure. She denied it all over the place. *Oh, no,* she said, *I'm just looking around, just straightening up. Don't mind me,* she said. I just went back and lay down again without

155

saying a word. To let her know I know what's going on.

She didn't make any noise out there for must have been near ten minutes. Then she came into the bedroom, me staring at the fan, one foot on the floor as I said. I expected her to fuss some more over me but you've got to give her credit because she didn't. She just looked at the ceiling fan with me for a few minutes with her one hand on her hip there. I glanced at her for a second. Saw she's shrunk a bit. Used to be taller, I'm sure of it.

After a while she sighed and said, *Well, Peter, it's a hard life.*

I let the arm of the fan that I had my eye on go around three more times before I looked at her in the doorway there.

Isn't it just, Lois. Isn't it just.

℘

Takealookattheboxfolks whatsit got Norm
holdituphighthere flowered bedsheets bedsheetsand
ballsayarn that'sadandyboxfolks wouldyalookat
*thecolours*inthatbox let'sstart'eratadollaronedollar
HEY'llyadbidwho'llyabiddollarabidnow
onebuckfolks andI'llthrowinthequiltingframehere
packagedeal onedollardollarabidwillyabidnow
c'monfolkswho'llgimmeonedollar dollarabid
overhereIhaveonedollarSOLD thankgodferthat

157

಄

A documentary on the radio about land mines and undetonated cluster bombs and the proliferation of small firearms on the world market. At the moment in the Sudan an AK47 goes for the price of a chicken. Late November. Sun sets early, leaving the whole city feeling low. Or maybe I'm projecting.

I go to the No Frills and, when I'm ready to pay, choose the longest line so that I can watch the habits of the other customers. Volumes of information in short exchanges between parents and their small children over whether or not they will buy one of the chocolate bars displayed at each checkout like a test. Information about who's got the power and whether it's stable and what tactics they rely on to maintain it. I stand in line and try to pinpoint the juncture where principles lose their foundations and slip into tactics. All in a glimpse at the gates of heaven.

The checkout girls banter with one another over our heads as if we were cattle waiting to be processed. Mine is a large-eyed dimpled South Asian girl whose black braid is thicker than my wrist. She moves languidly, as if in another set of stimuli altogether. Her braid reclines against her spine as she bends over to unclog the conveyor belt. Around me families bicker in their mother tongues and buy in bulk. I tenderly memorize everyone's groceries. I love the man in front of me for buying only plum sauce and cat food and loading them into his Labatt's Blue duffle bag. He has a plan which involves plum sauce. He changes the kitty litter. He finds ways to keep his spirits up.

I walk out into the 5 pm darkness with my purchases, the plastic bags cutting into my palms as I navigate the sidewalks home. In the Sudan an AK47 goes for the price of a chicken. I keep thinking that if I'm going to eat chicken I should raise and kill and pluck and cook one all by myself someday, but I doubt it will ever happen—more likely, my conscience will continue to let itself be soothed by the thinking of virtuous thoughts.

The street lights are on. Like nightlights for children afraid of the dark. Such thoughtful, coddling city planners.

❧

12 the canada goose (*branta canadensis*)

The November after Grandpa sells his house, he is almost
too depressed to speak. 150 km away I walk mornings by
the lake, angling for a glimpse of water only, wanting no city
anywhere, not even in periphery.

The Canada geese at the lakeshore in Toronto don't fly
south anymore—they stay, all winter, for tossed crusts.

The Canada geese at the lakeshore in Toronto don't fly
south anymore, don't get
                              hungry
             anymore.

~

These days I've got to make sure I'm holding onto something steady all the time. It's not just falling anymore. It's like the ground is sucking you down. Ever since I sold the house. Even on solid ground it's nip and tuck keeping your balance these days.

Well. Whatever else can be said about me, I still put on my own socks by God. Takes me ten goddamn minutes for each one. But I do it. I have this way of fixing them, bunching them up you know. I have to sit in that low chair. The one that came from the Dowswell place. And when I first bend over I have to rest there like that for a while. Give my blood a chance to get used to the arrangement. Blood's getting to be awfully finicky these days. Dizzy all the time. Doc says it's either a something or other in the ear or a brain tumour. Well I guess I like a straightforward man. So. I'm booked in to have a whadyacallit. A CAT scan. In January. The new year as they say. See if my brain is still there. Or if it's altogether dissolved. Wouldn't be surprised. What was I saying? Oh yes, so once I get my blood... acclimatized you might say, I can start to work it on. Goddamn fingers puffy good for nothing. Look at the things. Tires a man out when he's got all this useless flesh to look after. Can't even pull on a goddamn pair of socks without starting to bleed under the skin. There, like that. Look at them. Goddamn useless. Rotting. Wish they'd just rot right off some days and have it over with. See the trick is getting it over the heel. Goddamn feet more swollen than the goddamn fingers. I tried to use the shoehorn once but it gave me a bastard of a bruise. Well. Doesn't matter.

When I get the one sock on I take a rest. Lean back in the chair. And I sit there for a while with one sock on. I often think it'd make a funny picture. I mean if somebody came in on me then. Old geezer leaning back in his chair with his eyes closed and one sock on. And the sun not even up yet.

Anyhow. When my blood settles down I do it all over again. With the other foot.

Goddamn fingers. Sometimes I wonder why I bother. A man's got to wear socks though.

~

13 the cockatiel (*nymphicus hollandicus*)

My cousin Clara's triplets have turned two and she can't look after Sven, her cockatiel, so Grandpa is nominated to take the thing—a companion for Sandy, his canary.

He walks slowly around the seniors' complex on his way to visit Grandma in extended care, and the bird perches on his shoulder all the while, picks crumbs from the side of his mouth, pulls at his earlobe, shits down his back. In the Home he becomes known as the birdman, a claim to fame (though people talk even less to him now, too busy cooing to the bird).

The social coordinator is taken with it all, devises a contest to rename the cockatiel.

Perky
      is the winning entry, but Grandpa
calls him by no name,
coddles and curses him, chides him
if he hasn't sung a note by noon.

శ

Clara took back her cockatiel because of how much Grandpa complained about it, but then he seemed so depressed that Uncle Nick figured he'd better do something about it and gave him a bird clock for his birthday. The best of the best— mail-ordered from the Audubon Society. Twelve different birds, each perching at their appointed hour complete with English and Latin names. But the best part is the calls. The most realistic of any of the bird clocks, Nick was told. At one o'clock the house wren conjectures a long, almost haphazard line of thought on into the minute. At three o'clock the black-capped chickadee is matter-of-fact and predictable. Grandpa says the robin song at seven o'clock is the very essence of the hour after a spring storm, the worms surfacing and plentiful. I have to take his word for it; I never arrive as early as seven, never stay as late as seven. The place smells too intimate—skin gone loose and rubbery, pots of ointment long past their expiry dates—and after a couple of hours I'm ready for fresh air.

At noon and at midnight the owl sounds. Sitting down for lunch right under the clock in his small apartment yesterday, Grandpa opened his mouth to the sound of the noon-owl and, for a brief moment, I thought the moan was coming from him. The clock marked several minutes before my limbs stopped tingling and I could lift my fork, join him in eating the dinner he'd prepared: chicken roasted with onions and anise seed.

On the way home, I try not to imagine the owl-call at midnight. Grandpa, alone in his small apartment, upright, trying to fall asleep in the easy chair, opening his mouth in the dark. Behind him, chicken bones everywhichway in the wastebasket under the sink.

Holy mother how that bloody call lasts.

❧

When the one real bird that's left, the canary in the cage, begins to sing in his small apartment, Grandpa says, *Give 'er hell, Sandy.*

and to hold

☙

After a while we settle into a routine of visiting. Mom and I usually drive out together, have an early lunch with Grandpa, then walk over to Extended Care and feed Grandma her lunch. I often have to rush back to the city to work.

Whenever I have to work a shift at the bar after a visit with Grandma, I always feel like a foreigner in my life. Invariably I drift through the whole evening at a slight remove—*how odd, these people's customs*—though the distance is never quite as intense as it was the shift I worked after the day we moved her.

Suddenly it seemed a strange and unasked-for mission to move among the living and count out coins for change. To balance a cork tray stacked with empty glasses through the crowd then set it down on a gleaming copper pass-bar. Each customer impressed me: the act of choosing one beverage over another, the unlikely reliability of skin as a border to the body, the bravura of being out in public.

All night I watched them with the same gaze I'd levelled on Grandma all day.

Who knows her? What's he thinking? What's she loyal to? Does someone love him?

Love?

The band performed a disjointed sound check. A regular watched the hockey game on the TV above the bar, his face tracing a live map of passes, shots and saves.

What's it like to be inside that skull? To look out from behind those eyes? Inhabit that walk? That slouch?

Buddy in the corner had had one too many and his face

had slipped its anchor, was drifting out to sea.

What do we mean when we say we know a person?

How can we know anything?

Four people around a table all tipped their faces back to laugh as if opening a passage for some amber draught to pour into them from above.

Careful observation? Extrapolation? Imagination? Contemplation?

The music started in earnest and the drunk in the corner revived enough to heckle the band a little.

A good guess? A wild guess?

Love?

That word again.

The drunk lurched from his corner toward the door, calling over his shoulder, "Don't forget to laugh behind my back when I leave."

Unaware of him, the table of four laughed again, about something else.

And all night my mind kept stealing back to the window of her face, its kitchen curtains closed.

❧

James told me once that I almost always twitch just after I've fallen asleep. Not little twitches, he said—two or three leaping twitches, originating in the thigh, rabbits springing from the brush of my body. As if a starter pistol trigger has been pulled, as if I were leaving. It gives me an ache, this picture of him lying curled around me, his chest against my back, holding my body for me while I'm gone.

There are a handful of moments like that, which make it all seem worthwhile. *Beads of sensation*, Virginia Woolf called them. Making time stop flowing in just one direction, a vertical pressure felt against the horizontal, the pull of eternity. The moment breaks off, beads—a balanced sphere, a wobbling, tiny whole.

Then fill in the rest: distractions, defences, blame, bickering, pettiness, breaches of trust small and large, ego trips, expectations. Taking each other profoundly for granted. Knowing exactly what sentence will hurt the other most. The injustice of the fact that the one time you utter it outweighs by a long shot the thousand times you held your tongue. The morning breath. The shared popcorn. The silly dances while undressing. The customs your bodies develop while you sleep. Laziness. Irritability. Loneliness. Pride. The pause in lovemaking to remove a pubic hair from your tongue. Could you look at this thing on my back? Is it a zit or a bite or cancer?

It's such a strange thing, attention. How it can shift—past, present, future, there, elsewhere, everywhere—and all the while your body is here, your skin making contact with the air, parasites living their lives out in your eyelashes, maybe a cancer forming from the tiniest of cells in your left breast and ten years from now it will announce itself on the scene, finally getting your attention. And your elbow itches, and you scratch it with only a fraction of your attention, and the man you share a life with and say you love is reading to you from some dense philosophical text about pre-Cartesian conceptions of the Self, and part of your attention is with him but another part is thinking about the moment of peace you had this morning and how it seemed to you for a second that you didn't need to prove anything to anyone and how fleeting it was and what will you cook with the fish that needs to be used up, probably should have something green. He teases you about your need to have something green every day, how farmers used to eat greens every day in spring and summer then not at all during the winter, the two of you always trying out different angles for arriving at the most basic formula for a good human life and once you put it that way how absurd it sounds, but the compulsion is there and oh the ivy in the window needs watering and all the while he's reading to you about the Self and you realize you've only taken in a fraction and there's a swell of resentment because he never asks if he can read to you, does he? He just goes ahead and does it, walks into the room where you are working—you've established this before about when you're working—but he just walks into the room and says, *Listen to this*, but it would be more trouble than it was worth at the moment to take him to task over it—you know, because you've done it, because it would turn into a Big Deal (or is it just that you've never found the right way to do it?), and if you just listen (or half-listen or pretend to listen as you're doing now) it will be over sooner than a fight would be and, though you know there's a dishonesty in this, a shirking, you do it anyway because you're lazy.

My favourite moments are the ones when we laugh together in bed, gazing at each other from our pillows, inches from bridge of nose to bridge of nose. Those times we laugh at something inexplicably funny, something mild and silly, and the laughing doesn't match it—the laughing extends beyond the boundaries of the slight joke, makes little eaves, and the eaves gesture at sheltering all the sad-funny stuff of the whole day, though of course they can't. No one could recount or explain those moments—their humour doesn't last or translate—but I tell you they are my favourite times, my favourite.

Last week when I got back from visiting Grandma he told me if it happens to me when we get old, he'll keep trying to make me laugh.

I stroked his cheek, but to be honest it struck me as farfetched, and I just barely managed to keep from saying, *If we make it that long.*

﹏

My mother is president of the family reunion, whatever that means. She told me last night over the phone that when it came her turn to give the report on our branch of the family, she tried to be positive, said, "Mom doesn't talk or walk much anymore, but sometimes she seems to know us."

Lillian, Grandma's ever-catty cousin, stood up and said, "Well, I disagree with Ruth. I saw Mary two months ago, and she's just useless—she's a vegetable. I hope she dies quickly."

Mom said on the phone that the word *bitch* was in her mouth, but, like a good president, she swallowed it, finished chairing the meeting and went home before the potluck.

Her voice on the phone sounded peculiar, drained. Though she didn't say and I didn't ask, I bet she cried in the car on the way home, cried harder than that particular incident warranted, cried long. I have an image of her sobbing so hard she had to pull the car over. I bet the crying just kept coming, like a bottle of homemade wine aged to vinegar chugging slowly out of the bottleneck into the earth in the backyard.

ॐ

In early December the zoo is deserted. James and I spend a long time watching the hippos swim under water. Something presumptuous about peering through an underground window at very large animals paddling and gliding, something too intimate.

We walk and James talks to me about how Plato, in the *Timaeus*, investigates the essential nature of things, their origins. I take it in obliquely. Something about atomic structure of the elements as geometry. Earth is cube-shaped. Fire is scalene-triangle-shaped; it's pointiest, that's why it burns. Space is a grand receptacle and it shakes us like a winnowing basket so that like-shaped particles congregate. There is no such thing as above and below, only centres and peripheries, overlapping, only like things massing together and attracting their fellows to their gathering.

Sometimes lately I'm afraid that marrying so young has stunted me somehow, made me odd, unfit for modern life. I can't decide whether I'm extremely loyal or extremely clingy, can't tell the difference between beauty and pathology.

Often lately a feeling of the timing being off between us, but combined with an urgency—like we're running a three-legged race and have forgotten to have fun, are focused only on the finish line.

He wants us to have a baby. No pressure, not necessarily right now, but he wants us to start thinking about it. Right now the thought makes me feel swallowed whole.

I'd like to explain zoos in terms of cubes and triangles, angles and attractions. I would like to explain terrorism, romance and regret. Bewilderment for days on end. Underwater zoo animals never giving you more than a glimpse of themselves, sticking to the other end of the pool. James complains that I'm distant, flat. I drive us home in a borrowed car. Follow the traffic signs. Right turn, round steering wheel, parallel parking. The geometry of the meantime.

❧

Grandma can't feed herself anymore, and Mom and I have found that feeding her gives the visit a focus, even though it's depressing. They serve everything puréed in Extended Care. Lunch menu for today: puréed ham sandwich. Dinner: puréed roast beef with puréed Yorkshire pudding.

One day, I'm holding a spoonful of applesauce in the air, waiting for Grandma to finish swallowing the one before, and Mom says, "If it happens to me you have to promise you'll make sure to feed me a little of everything in each bite."

We've always teased Mom about how she eats. Whatever's on her plate—roast beef, mashed potatoes, carrots, peas— she takes some of each in each bite, the mounds shrinking proportionately throughout the meal, always attentive, evening it out, taking a bit more potato with one bite if necessary, timing it so that the final bite will have a little of everything.

I laugh and say, "Sure Mom." But when I look at her, she isn't laughing. She drops her eyes and, after a moment, picks up one of Grandma's hands.

"How *do* your fingernails get so dirty?" she coos.

Another day, we're driving home together from the nursing home. She's offered to drive me all the way back into the city, drop me off at my place. Traffic is sparse. As we near the exit she breaks the silence, says, "Well if it happens to me I just hope to God I have the courage to drive myself off a bridge."

I look at her. She looks at the road. Her hands tight at ten and two on the steering wheel.

❧

There was a story that fascinated me, one I latched onto
from Mom's growing up. I don't remember in what context
Mom told it to me; it's not really even much of a story, more
an image: Grandma waiting behind the curtains for Mom to
come home from her dates. She'd wait and wait and watch
the chaste kiss on the front porch and then slap Mom's face
when she got inside. That was it. That image explained why
Mom couldn't wait to leave. Why she didn't come home for
a long time after she left for university and why she began
going back only gradually. Then more and more when I was
born. I wonder if back then she could have imagined herself
going every weekend to iron labels into the inside collar of all
her mother's blouses, write her name in indelible markers on
the soles of all her shoes, Mary Friesen Mary Friesen Mary
Friesen, getting her ready to go to the Home.

I remember one of those weekends in particular. Mom
ensconced herself in the bedroom sorting girdles and slips.
I stayed in the living room with Grandma, who was on the
couch reading aloud the same section about a bear attack
over and over again from a *Reader's Digest*. At one point, out
of the blue, she looked up, saw Mom's purse on the coffee
table and said, "Whose purse is that?"

"It's my mom's purse, Grandma. Your daughter—Ruth's
purse."

"Ruth is here?"

"Yep, in the bedroom."

"For a visit?"

"Yes, for a visit."

"Isn't that lovely," she said, struggling up from the couch, and went to the back of the house to greet her daughter.

A few minutes later, settled again on the couch, reading and rereading a similar paragraph from later in the same article, she looked up.

"Whose purse is that?" she said. "Is someone here?"

"Ruth is here," I said.

"How lovely! For a visit?"

And again the joyous greeting in the bedroom was re-enacted. I watched Mom. It was as if by chance she'd taken a simple step aside and missed the usual landslide of bleak discomfort and undiscussed grief, was able to simply put down what she was doing and greet her mother with open, empty arms. All three of us rose, as if through a lesser gravity, to the occasion. We even laughed, playing it up a little, letting Grandma have her day in the sun, letting her lead us through the tender surprise of visitation over and over again, all through the afternoon, like a dish of candies too sweet for you to keep your hand from drifting back.

෨

James and I watched a film last week, an arty one with a
score by Philip Glass and a foreign title I can't remember but
which translated as *Life Out of Balance*. I've been haunted by
one of the images from it ever since: a panning aerial shot of
acres and acres of abandoned apartment buildings.

They exist somewhere in the world, I guess, standing there
empty. But it felt like watching a prophecy.

❧

On the subway, afternoon rush hour. I've read all the advertisements, so I play one of my little games. Today it's guessing whether people are single or not just by the way they carry themselves, seeing if you can read the joining of lives on a body.

Suddenly the subway slows and stops mid-tunnel. People groan and look up from their newspapers and paperbacks, look around over each other's heads out into the blackness of the tunnel. Some people catch each other's eyes and shrug—these are the naturally gregarious ones, or the ones born elsewhere.

Nothing to do but wait. After a few minutes, a voice comes to us over the speaker system. Presumably, the voice is explaining the reason for the delay, but the words are scattered and flattened by the speaker system. We look around at each other again, puzzled. As far as I can tell from the body language of the others, no one was able to make out anything from the announcement beyond the weary, superior and slightly defensive tone of official apology.

Ten minutes pass. People gradually begin to talk with one another about connections they're going to miss, daycares that charge a dollar for every minute you're late.

I'm thinking it was a jumper.

After twenty minutes I turn to the woman next to me and say, "How about you?" She's older than I am, but younger than my mother. Her hair dyed blonde, but not platinum—a dirty blonde trying to match an old natural. Homemade-looking scarf, practical boots.

"How about me what?" she says, but in an inviting way. She has an accent. European. I like the lines around her eyes—they seem to suggest a habitual expression of tender commiseration.

"Are you going to be late for something?"

She looks at her watch as if it's just occurred to her. "Oh, maybe. But I always give myself plenty of time to get to work. Just in case." She says this not without a note of smugness in her voice, like the ant to the grasshopper. The self-satisfied voice of the citizen who has forgone her allotment of summer fun in order to stockpile for the hardships ahead.

"What do you do?" I ask, grateful to have a natural opening for the question. It's the question we always want to ask. Not to place someone in the class structure anymore—which is the old and valid objection to the question—but because we're genuinely curious. I always stop myself from asking though, because what if the person is out of work or can't tell by my tone that I think all work is valuable?

"I'm in meat inspection," she says. No nonsense. Matter of fact. This, I think, is a woman who faces facts. A woman who has seen people break promises and die untimely deaths, a woman who has cleaned up unspeakable messes.

"Ah," I say, "meat inspection."

"Chickens," she says, nodding, looking at her hands. "At a kosher chicken plant in North York. It's hard on your body, standing like that all the day long. And on your hands. Hard on your hands, I mean."

We sit side by side in silence for a while as I take this in.

"Thirty-eight a minute," she says. And it takes me a moment to realize she's talking chickens. That this woman earns her living inspecting thirty-eight chickens a minute. All the day long.

"It's better than some places. I worked in one company that did eighty-six a minute. They did it electronically with x-ray cameras, one person looking at the viscera, another at the cavity and so on. Me I do it by hand now." She gestures as if opening a book with her thumbs. "Open each one up."

"Wow," I say. I try to think of something else to say but am stumped. My social graces have for the moment been swept away on a wave of generalized guilt. Guilt for my eating of chickens, guilt for my comparatively cushy work. This woman has a kindness about her that makes me afraid for her.

"I'm getting older, and I'm on my own since my marriage ended and I don't know how much longer I can do it. I hate these night shifts especially. I want to try to get an office position in the company, but it's exactly how they say. I didn't believe it at first, but I know now it's true. It's who you know, you know. And people are so backbiting. It's unbelievable, but you have to believe it."

Her accent is lovely. The way she says *unbelievable* is so pristine, the word sounds as if it were doing a high platform dive with a twist from her lips.

The subway jerks forward, the obstruction having apparently been addressed.

ॐ

I'm tired all the time lately. Sandbags in my limbs keeping a flood at bay. I refuse to use the word depressed. The word depressed depresses me.

I walk around thinking, *I'm not included*. I watch the perpetual impromptu yard sales spread out on the wide patch of sidewalk just east of the No Frills by the newspaper boxes. I watch the pigeons take off and land, take off and land and I think, *I am not included in the life of this sidewalk*. A pigeon on the ledge of a boarded-over window on the Bingo Country building gazes at me from behind another pigeon and moves its head to one side as if to say, *Meet me in the other room so I can tell you a secret*. I keep walking.

A couple in the window of the café where I stop to have a coffee is kissing in the full sunlight, heads rotating this way and that, sucking face as if milking each other for all they're worth. *I'm not included*, I think. I try to think it without the self-pity, see if it can still be thought. It can, but it's different: colder, limpid, almost philosophical. *Not included*.

From time to time Sammy, the bartender I work with every Friday night, will write *Get a room* on a chit and slip it nonchalantly, as if it's their bill, onto the table of a couple who starts fondling each other at the bar. Sometimes they laugh when they read it; sometimes they don't.

He says he figures the couples who laugh will be the ones who last.

~

Connie

Early retirement I call it. Cheques come from welfare end of the month and Billy signs his over right away and I cash the both of them and cover the rent and the bills and head to the beer store with the empties and some cash, stock up for the month. I sublet the upstairs to a couple of old fairies and I make sure I get their rent off them before they liquefy their assets if you know what I'm saying. Next thing I head to the Market. Kensington. I know everybody in the Market and they all know me—been going there for twenty-five years now, even lived there for a bit, after my stint at Rochdale in the sixties. Cheapest chicken parts in the city if you know where to go. Spices in bulk. Fresh eggs, fresh fish. Whatever you want. Good stuff. All cheap. And I volunteer two days a week at the food bank—the big Daily Bread warehouse downtown—and they let me take the cream of the pickings there. Sometimes if they've got a big load of something good—like that time with the tubs of ricotta cheese just past their best-before—I take enough to share with the neighbours. And I got a garden out back. Save the seeds every fall in egg cartons, labelled. Start the seedlings inside in Styrofoam cups from the soup kitchen the food bank runs. I got a used freezer from the Buy-and-Sell a few years ago, so I can grow enough tomatoes for the whole year. I stake them up with the posts from campaign lawn posters—spent the morning after the election one year going around with my bundle-buggy, gathering them up. A few pot plants in between the tomatoes and no one's the wiser. The girl next door, she lent me her food dehydrator this year. It dried the weed up perfect in less than a day. I had her in to thank her, gave her a beer, smoked her up. I hinted how I've been hearing her and her man fighting lately. Then I got up and went to the fridge and cracked a couple more beers open and stood in front of her and before I handed hers down to her I looked at her and said in a slow voice, *When things get tough between a woman and a man, the woman's got to take a step back and ask herself, What's really going on here? What's really going on.* I don't figure she caught my drift, but at least I did my bit. Crazy how we're all a lot more likely to learn how to take care of a thing by killing it a few times than by just watching it grow. Who knows why, but that's how we're made, that much is for sure. I figure I've got a few things figured out by now. Enough anyhow for me and Billy to have a pretty good living.

꙳

Usually when James and I are in a disagreement we don't really fight—we freeze each other out. Mutual policy of strict sanctions: no smiles, no humour, no touch. Curt conversations, strictly logistical. Did you call the landlord about the furnace? What day is recycling now? Are we still going to your sister's on Sunday?

It never lasts long. Neither of us can stand it. Always the gradual thaw and before you know it we're lovers again. It occurred to me the other day though that lately the thaw hasn't been going quite through before the next freeze sets in, resulting in a kind of underground permafrost that you wouldn't notice unless you were digging. Plus sometimes we're actually out and out fighting. Funny thing is, I couldn't even really tell you what we're fighting about. Sometimes I hear myself saying we need to spend more time together. Sometimes I hear myself saying I need space. Sometimes I hear him saying I'm needy. Sometimes I hear him saying I'm cold. Neither of us wants to be fighting, but we can't seem to help ourselves.

Life out of balance. James and I have lost the flow in our economy. Somehow we've started tallying. We're competing to get where we used to compete to give.

Last night it escalated into a shouting match. At some point James grabbed his coat and went out for a walk to cool down. I turned on the stereo far louder than strictly recommended in the interest of good neighbourly relations. Dylan, *Desire*. I paced. I checked the messages. One from Gloria asking if I'll water her plants and feed her cat for the three weeks she's away over Christmas. Saying I can use the place to write in if I want.

I started to pack.

༄

I stand at Gloria's fifth-storey window and look out over the rooftops in the twilight. I love the flocks of pigeons in this grove of apartment buildings; whatever music I have on Gloria's stereo, they seem to be taking off and landing in time to it.

James and I are taking a break; no one to tell the day to.

The band that played at the bar last night finished their last set with a languid wander through "I'm So Lonesome I Could Cry." The percussionist—who'd been playing a cheese-grater earlier in the evening—played a solo on a toothless saw with a violin bow.

I think of my grandfather in his new apartment an hour and a half away. Stewing in a loneliness so intense and undeserved it borders on rage. How the equation is impossible: the greater the loneliness, the less eager I am to approach it.

On the streetcar this afternoon during rush hour I ended up wedged with my bags in a window seat by a large Portuguese widow, all in black. (How many years will she end up wearing black in comparison to the years she was married? Another impossible equation.) She had even more bags than I did. I always carry lots of bags. Big purse. Backpack. Plastic shopping bags. Library books, errands, changes of clothes just in case. James calls me Baglady, a term of endearment. I don't let him use regular terms of endearment. Honey, sweetie. They make me feel like a caricature of a couple, they make me feel in danger of disappearing. James is disheartened by this but goes along, which makes me feel both cruel and

crazy in love with him. He's become inventive. *Problem-child,*
he calls me. *My velour kitten,* he calls me when I wear my blue
hoodie. *Mmm,* I say, *rub me the wrong way.*

Hey Baglady, he calls me.

The freefall of every second. On the streetcar, crowded
with my bags beside the Portuguese widow, I sat watching
us all—passengers, passive. Wanting to know how to never,
never kill time.

❧

Insomnia. I check the mirror in Gloria's bathroom: looks like I spent all night reading the newspaper then rubbed the ink on my fingertips off under my eyes.

Middle finger of my right hand throbbing where I caught it in the faulty fan of the beer fridge at work. Throbbing in time to my heartbeat. Hard not to think fuck you fuck you fuck you.

Insomnia is like being caught in a sieve when all you want to do is be liquid and fall through. I try different positions. Stomach, side, back, other side, foetal, stretched, two pillows, one pillow, none. I get up to get a glass of water. An hour and a half later I get up to pee the water out. I switch on the light and read Lorca in New York ranting through his heartbreak about how the city can't receive morning how nothing is hallowed amid the greedy towers how we have let our bodies lose their auras. He couldn't sleep either.

I flip onto my stomach. Been thinking lately about the welfare state. I've been thinking about the institution of marriage and seatbelt laws and the granting of bachelor degrees. About life as a series of shams of safety. Universal healthcare is undoubtedly a good thing. And yet, I've begun to wonder if the social safety net has, on some fundamental level, made me a softie. Oh lord. Am I becoming a redneck? What is a redneck anyway? Someone who works bent over in the sun.

I can feel myself veering with the stubbornness of a shopping cart with a frozen wheel toward nihilism. It takes everything I have to counter the momentum, keep myself on track. I could volunteer somewhere but what good would that do? Charity is institutionalized pity. If only there were a barn-raising to attend. A crop to harvest. Yeah, right. If only I weren't such a bloody romantic. If only I could sleep. I flip onto my back, the covers twisted, pillow damp. Maybe insomnia is a product of capitalism. Or the industrial revolution. So simplistic. And yet...

All night my mind going like it's pedalling in too low a gear, going like it's trying to whip cream.

❧

To Mom's for Christmas dinner. James has come with me, but we're stiff. My mother has just had new white carpets laid in her house. White. Why on earth would a person choose white carpets? For Christmas, my stepfather gets her a cordless iron that turns itself off. She says, "I hope it didn't cost too much."

I've offered to put together the traditional basket of cheeses and preserves to bring to Aunt Deborah and Uncle Nick's. Later she says the basket looks nice. "You're good at that," she says. "You're not as stingy as I am."

We meet eyes.

It shocks me sometimes. Not the fact that I love her, but that I forget.

Gloria's building seems to have an unlimited hot water
supply and her utilities are included in her rent, so I'm taking
advantage while I'm here. I run a bath right to the top, hot as
I can stand it.

I've lit candles but don't have enough of them to read by
so have to switch the overhead light back on. You'd think
there'd be more light with the candles, but somehow there's
less; they take the edge off the glare of the glass-shaded bulb
screwed into the ceiling. I read until the bath is lukewarm
and the story—*The Death of Ivan Illich*—is finished and my
fingertips are puffy and wrinkled and then I sit for a while
longer, feeling clammy and blue, and indulge in a little private
wallowing. Time is passing. The bath is cooling. I'm getting
older by the second.

I stare at my fingertips and imagine my body fifty years
from now—when it's like Liza's or Mavis's or Grandma's.
When I'm pushing eighty will there be anyone in my life
with enough history with my body to love it for the story it
tells? I don't allow myself to think of the specificity of James'
body. The calluses on his chording fingers. The hair starting
to grow on his shoulders. His shoulders.

Any moment now I'll make the effort, lift myself out of
the bathwater, stand naked, briefly streaming like a cataract,
then bend, pull the plug, step out. But not yet. I'm not done
wallowing.

Is it okay to be lonely? Is it permissible? Or is it a sign of
a lack in me that should be addressed. Maybe the intensity
of my loneliness when I'm away from James proves me to be

backward, like a country whose people haven't yet learned to govern themselves, a country that still longs for a king. I sit in the cooling bath and look at the blue bathroom tiles, at the shapely white porcelain of the toilet. How does matter hold its form? There are very basic things I have no idea about. I sit in the bath and stare at the tall white candles burning at half-mast in Gloria's brass flea-market candelabra. What is it in us that craves intimacy? Is it that I want distraction? Is it simply the biological urge to procreate?

Or is it—please let it be—something indescribable. Something more.

❧

A conversation between regulars, overheard at the bar:

"You ever spent so long at your computer you find yourself sitting at the bar or on the streetcar expecting little drop-menus to come down in front of you?"

"I know whereof you speak, man. You spend all day working on an image file then work on it more at night asleep and then wake up and go to work and can't remember what you've done and haven't done. It's like a revolving door you can't get out of."

I stand behind the bar listening, sipping beer from a mug. Bartenders aren't, of course, supposed to drink on the job but dark beer looks remarkably like a latte when it's in a coffee mug. Listening, I'm washed by mild relief that other people feel that way too. The relief ebbs quickly, though, and is replaced by a deep undertow of dismay—dismay at the thought that being stuck in a metaphysical revolving door is normal.

Spit me out, I keep saying into the darkness. I don't know if it's prayer or demon-taming or superstition. I don't know if we are all fundamentally alone or fundamentally loved. I find I don't know a thing.

I sit on the streetcar these days and simmer in envy. I watch a mother two seats up nuzzling her toddler nose to nose, giggling, tickling—they're like lovers, except they need no privacy. A low low boil in me, a thickening liquid. Every once in a while a languid pop.

I close my eyes. Spit me out. I think I used to have something like faith. I vaguely remember having some kind of faith in something. No doubt it was misguided, but it seems to me it felt good at the time.

Give me some of that, I think. Some good old-fashioned feel-good faith.

I open my eyes and look out the streetcar window: a bearded man in an apron and short-sleeved t-shirt carrying stacked flats of eggs down the snowy sidewalk. Beaming. Dozens and dozens of eggs in his tattooed arms. Beaming.

And I grin in spite of myself.

～

Addicted to Tolstoy lately. I'm a sucker for his impossible
blend of moralistic romanticism and brute realism. Plus, *War
and Peace* is quite simply a page-turner. Who knew?

When I'm caught with a stranger in the elevator in Gloria's
building I can't help thinking about the peasant Nikita from
the story *Master and Man* who, from kind-hearted politeness,
always says something to anyone he's alone with. In the
elevator, I try at least to meet eyes, nod. It's exhausting. So
many people. Some of them unwilling to meet you halfway,
stonily thwarting your noble effort. Some of them too
willing, bottomless pits. Makes me want to hole up in the
apartment and never come out.

A five-storey building of bachelor apartments, twenty
apartments on each floor. When in human history have
people lived alone like this unless they were hermits or
outcasts?

I take a walk by the lake. When I get back to the building,
I decide to take the stairs, both for the exercise and to avoid
having to small-talk in the elevator.

There's a guy in the stairwell playing his guitar. I climb
into his sound. He's singing a song with a chorus about the
grand design. *You go your way and I'll go mine. Ah, the grand
design. . .* He stops playing as I pass.

"Great acoustics in here," he says, shy.

And, feeling genuinely sociable for the first time in weeks,
I say, "I'll say."

๛

Every Tuesday at the nursing home, Liza's nephew signs her out for dinner and returns her twenty minutes late for her scheduled bath. She and I small-talk as I soap her back. Tonight Liza can't remember the name of the restaurant but remembers they got lost on the way. Can't remember what she had for dinner but remembers—quite emphatically— that it was delicious. I smile, though to be honest the better part of me is already home, book in hand, cat in lap.

When I do get home, the cat won't settle, noses my book, kneads my thighs, sniffs my tea, turns round and round as if to rouse or quell some invisible vortex. I stare at the ceiling— the cat's tail swishing in my face, her asshole a repellent pink pucker, her purr infuriating—and picture myself at work, capable, needed, irreproachably earning my keep.

It's not lost on me, the absurdity of bathing other people's grandparents for a living while other people bathe mine. The disconnect there too far gone to be reasonably mourned. A whole economy wedged in the gap.

Sorry, I say to Liza, when the water's too hot or too cold. She looks up. *Oh, no worry, it's neither here nor there.*

Last night I forgot to put the milk back in the fridge. This morning it clots uncooperatively in my hot tea. I know if I were to make a new cup and drink it clear, I'd drink it thinking, *I should have just gone to the corner store.* So I go to the store thinking, *I should have just had it clear.* I pay for the milk with a painstaking pocketful of nickels and dimes, the cashier looking over my shoulder as I count, and head home cradling the carton in the crook of my arm, a tipped column of sloshing white liquid, miles and miles from the nearest milk cow. I try briefly as I walk to burrow under the surface of the moment but immediately hit bedrock.

Outside Holy Family Catholic Church a woman squats on the sidewalk, back against the wall, panhandling—hairy-chinned, an air of contagion—my eyes at once drawn and spurned by hers as I pass. I raise my gaze. The signboard outside the church suggests I *go forth, be fruitful and multiply*.

My cousin Clara has what I think of as a knack for life, her uncanny power for spotting four-leafed clovers a case in point. Give her an hour on a lawn, she'll pluck a dozen—no kidding—and I can't even find one. When she and her juggler/psychiatrist husband found they couldn't conceive, they turned to technology. All three eggs took and, when doctor offered the irrefutable advice that it would be better to abort the weakest, she refused. So now Clara is the mother of triplets.

Harrowing how each *yes* seems to call for *yeses* in triplicate, *yeses* rivering outward, exponential.

Years ago, when Grandma was drawing up the family tree, Grandpa made an uncharacteristic stand: he refused to let her leave off the childless divorces as if they'd never happened. How I love him for that, for preserving the branches that seemed to lead nowhere.

Most mornings I walk by the lake. I have to cross the expressway to get there (the on-ramps and off-ramps sketching compulsive cloverleafs). Last Christmas, having just seen ultrasound images of her mother's cancer (all the veins drawing from the surrounding cells to feed the tumour) Gloria said that flying into Toronto (all the roads drawing from the countryside to feed the city), she couldn't help but think.

Something hisses under my skin these days, insistent, like the Freon that time I was impatient and used an ice pick to defrost my fridge.

Catching me steal a look at my watch while I'm waiting for him to manoeuvre his walker into position, Fred, the brain-injured man I shower on Wednesdays, says to me, *Is it now?*

Mornings by the lake, I think about the word *design*, about the organic nature of even the least organic thing, about the ancient story in which Love is the bastard child of Resource and Poverty, about the symmetrical helplessness of infants and elders. The on-ramp and off-ramp of each life: disability. And in between?

Can't help feeling that somewhere we've missed a connection.

Did I mention what it said on the hand-lettered sign held by the woman on the sidewalk?

Spare some change or I'll touch you.

~

Love?

Though we all know the word is distended and threadbare
with too many wearings and mendings and bleachings and
though lately the moral of each day's story seems to come
back to how impossible it is to know another person and
though I could very easily be deluding myself, I think maybe
just maybe I might be feeling the shape of it rising in me
lately like a kind of groundwater ever-so-slowly by fractions
and increments

toward places I hadn't expected to feel it. And it's not at all
romantic. It's

terrifying. I think of him taking care of her all those months
of her decline. A river draining, emptying faster than it fills.
Somewhere else, in some realm I can't see,

a flood.

Mother, I want to take your hand from the steering wheel.
Hold onto it for

dear life. I want to feed you a little of

everything.

࿊

things that still have not left her (2)

1
chewing
with her mouth closed

2
smiling
when kissed

❧

The other day I went to the hospital with Grandpa for his cataract operation. Mom and Uncle Nick, being teachers, both had to work, but my schedule is flexible so I said sure.

Two older women in the waiting room were talking about the weather. They seemed strangers but had somehow managed to strike up a conversation. Normally I could just ignore that sort of thing—*blah, blah, blah, retirement communities, blah blah blah, bladder control, blah blah blah, can you believe Christmas is over already oh well it'll be back before you know it*—but for some reason, maybe because I was slightly hungover and had forgotten to bring a book, that day I couldn't stand it. Their conversation wasn't *going* anywhere. It was all I could do to keep from leaning over and telling them to just *shut up*. I actually had to get up and go to the washroom.

When I came back from the washroom I paused in the doorway for a moment and looked at them—seated side by side, turned slightly toward each other but still facing forward, staring at their clasped hands or at the floor, taking turns speaking and nodding. And I got it: old ladies in waiting rooms speak a dying language, the subtleties of which can easily pass you by.

What they're really saying is:

it's important
that we be civil to each other

yes,   *I believe in that*

memory may go but the details
are still
important

I agree   the details
are important

❦

I lie in Gloria's bed thinking how I want to be less predictable, more various and flexible and hospitable to surprise. I want to have many children and live in a shoe and somehow manage. I've been thinking I need to say *no* more often, but really I want to say *yes*. I want to be inconvenient and alive. I want to have a one-night stand tonight with my husband of seven years. I want to seduce him.

The city makes a hollow roaring sound around the apartment, like something large and empty exhaling endlessly.

What have I done with these years? Always reserving part of myself from any one thing—art, work, politics, my relationships—just in case. Afraid I won't receive the recognition I need in order to justify spending myself fully. Always keeping back a nest-egg, a private little hoard of self.

I'll go home in the morning.

I lay waiting for the night to be over, heavy-limbed with the thought that it could be too late.

~

James and I go out, just the two of us, the way we used to when we first met. We choose a pub out of the neighbourhood, a place with good nachos, where it's unlikely we'll run into anyone we know. I can tell he's making as much of an effort as I am. We're careful with each other, but not in a bad way, not in an edgy, stepping-on-eggshells way. More in a reverent, careful-with-the-newborn way.

He asks me about the writing I did at Gloria's. I tell him I'm trying to get over my embarrassment about how tame and domestic it all is. "Guess there's just something compelling to me about the mundane," I say.

He considers for a moment then says, "I think in an ideal world we'd each have our own bard."

I laugh and sip my beer, thinking how wrong-headed my *need some space* instinct is—it's when we *don't* spend time together that things go wrong. On the other hand, would I have been able to see this without having taken the space?

"Think about it," he says. "Every single person on the planet with his or her very own personal bard, the way Celtic chieftains all had a bard in their entourage. A guy with a lute slung across his chest, following each and every one of us around, composing lyrics about our every little triumph and defeat."

"Yeah, the mountain of dishes conquered, the battle of the diaper change won but the war grinding on."

"Exactly! Imagine—each paper cut and parking ticket properly lamented. A whole song for your new hairdo. A whole song for the day when you were a kid and you ran away from home and no one noticed and when you came home your goldfish was belly up in the fishbowl and your mother had made liver for dinner."

"A whole song for the first kiss," I add, "and the bard plays it in the background every time you kiss anyone after that. With appropriate variations, of course. And a whole song for the first fight. The first fight preserved in all its agonizing detail."

James and I meet eyes across the table.

"But at the same time," he says, "the whole thing sung in metred verse—as if it couldn't have gone down in any other way."

We're quiet a moment, eyes locked.

Then the moment passes. The waitress comes and we order two more pints. I decide I don't care how I'll feel tomorrow. I decide I love everything about this night. Every last detail.

❧

Some days I can almost understand
why she might want to forget it all—
like the temptation when carrying a
heavy load, a load too big for your
arms, to drop the whole thing rather than
choose
            what to put down,
what to carry on. So much to hold

like how the day of the spontaneous watermelon seed contest
—*Who can spit one into the bird bath first?*—

was the same day Grandpa told us he was going to sell the house

and how, when my stepfather brought back cigars from
Cuba, one for everyone, Grandpa saved his for his birthday,
kept it in the fridge, folded in a plastic milk bag with a stub
of carrot, *to keep it fresh*

and how, when I brought him the little mason jar full of
cherries that I had dried in his machine, he said, *Are they the
sour or the sweet? Sour*, I said, and he smiled—*Just the thought and
I can feel it in here*, he said, rubbing his jawbone

and the note he wrote in block letters on cardboard and put
with the dryer when he sent it with Mom:

THIS DEHYDRATOR IS TO GO TO MY GRANDDAUGHTER
UNLESS SHE ISN'T INTERESTED ENOUGH IN IT
AND THEN I'LL SELL IT

and in smaller letters:
(AND I'M GOING TO ASK FOR $100
BECAUSE IT COST A LOT MORE THAN THAT
WITH THE ATTACHMENTS)

and how, when we were visiting one weekend Grandpa peeled a banana and fed it to Grandma and Mom said to him, *Do you remember how you used to always both bring home bananas on the same day?*

and later, when Mom went out to get groceries for him, he brought out his electric razor, held Grandma's face steady and her shaved chin, rubbing her jawbone and saying, *There, now she looks respectable*

and when we were cleaning out the basement for the auction I found a shoebox labelled, *strings too short to be of use*

and how Grandma's house was always full of candy dishes, how her bevelled-glass candy dishes always had candy

and Grandma pulling out her empty pockets at Thanksgiving dinner, saying, *I want to show you something*

and how, when she no longer lived in her house, my grandmother's candy dishes had wood screws and pill bottles and fertilizer sticks for violets, and when they had candy it was sticky and stale and didn't come properly out of the wrapper

and how, when watering the violets on the window sill, Grandpa said the grosbeaks get drunk on crabapples in late autumn, *after they've got a couple frosts on 'em*

and how Uncle Nick brought beer, and Grandpa said he
might just get drunk for his eighty-seventh birthday

but he never did

and how he never smoked that cigar either

and how Grandpa said Aunt Dorothy giggled over
Grandma's new Denby Twilight dish set, how he knew what
she was going to say before she said it: *The teacups are shaped
like chamber pots!*

and all I know about Aunt Anne is that she was Grandpa's
favourite sister and hated blue jays because they were greedy
at her feeder

and though everything I thought I knew about what makes a life
is getting smaller and
smaller, lighter and
lighter, I seem to be less
and less able to
hold it all.

~

details from the urban soundscape

1

One morning last winter, I was woken by the squealing sound of a car spinning its wheels in a snowbank outside. The car digging itself deeper and deeper into hysteria.

I'd been having trouble getting out of bed in the mornings. The whining engine—the sound of no-traction panic—must have been burrowing into my half-consciousness for some time before it finally broke through and made me throw off the covers. And, no kidding, the very moment my feet hit the floor the squealing stopped, tires caught, engine engaged, the car drove off and I stood there, suddenly hungry

for the day.

2

Many of the major intersections downtown now have chirping bird noises so the blind know when to cross the street—a perky go-ahead chirp for the north-south axis and a lower, slower chirp for east-west.

Would the two sounds be identifiable to someone more literate in the language of birdcall? Or are they shorthand cartoons of birdsong, the way the lit-up walking stick-man of the visual pedestrian signal is shorthand for human?

Does the call and response of the intersections confuse the real birds?

3

In the middle of the night, sirens swoop in my neighbourhood like mosquitoes around the head of a sleeper in a tent, closer then farther. Fluctuations of an everlasting emergency. Just when you think they've died down, they return, sirens right inside your ear, impossible to swat.

4

In line at the bank downtown, transferring my weight from one foot to the other on the cool, hard marble floors, high-ceilinged hush of held breath, everybody behaving themselves in the belly of the beast. Somebody's cellphone rings behind me, and it sounds like the bank has been infiltrated by crickets.

5

Woken from a deep sleep by a storm last summer, James and I turned our heads on our pillows, met eyes during a lightning flash. His hand found mine under the covers. James is afraid of thunder. It's a fear I don't share, so I have to prompt myself to empathize. We didn't speak. My thumb stroked his. Lying there, we listened to the storm approaching from across the city until the thunder and lightning were almost simultaneous and they gave my heart a new pace and suddenly my forced empathy broke through, ran fresh.

And then, somewhere in the neighbourhood, a car alarm began to sound, set off by the flash and crack.

Which made me, for that moment, inexplicably happy.

6

Though I've never heard it myself, I'm told that residents of the neighbourhood bordering High Park sometimes hear coyotes howling in the distance.

7

Window open, early morning. Again, I'm woken from a deep sleep. This time by the sound of keening, many female voices wailing in unison from the apartment building across the street. I lie there blinking, disoriented. My body scoured by the women's voices. Somebody has just received a call from overseas maybe. Whatever it is, it's bad news. The women wail with both abandon and skill, communicating the fact of a loss, getting into all its corners, tunnelling through it so thoroughly it's linked to all loss, which makes it at once infinitely sadder and somehow easier to bear.

Then a single voice from the same building—somebody leans out from his balcony and yells:

WILL YOU SHUT THE FUCK UP IT'S FIVE O'CLOCK IN THE FUCKING MORNING TAKE YOUR MISERY SOMEPLACE ELSE

And the keening stops.

8

Most of the time you don't hear it, or not exactly. It blends into the background. It *is* the background, and you don't hear it, not as itself.

But sometimes you do hear it—especially late late at night or early early in the morning. Or, more specifically,

in that still-dark hour that's both late and early, that hour
just before dawn when you're, say, making your way home
slightly drunk from a night out—seeing a friend's band then
dancing at an after-hours booze-can—and you pass a group
of new immigrants (these ones look mostly Tibetan) on the
corner of King and Wilson Park, climbing one by one into
the Rent-a-Worker van that will take them to a factory on
the industrial outskirts of the suburbs where they'll trim the
loose threads from floor mats destined for Hondas all day
long, and the sight of them sobers you just enough to take in
the strangeness of the hour. It's then

you hear the sound itself: the drone of the city, its main
ingredient the traffic of the expressway, that prolonged

whoosh. But also, somewhere behind that, a blurred and
hard-to-get-at current. It's a sound as constant and pulsing
with force as surf, or a high strong wind in a mountain pass.
As I said, it's mostly traffic. Transport trucks careening
obediently between A and B along major arteries. A ghostly
sound, almost

otherworldly. Listening to it, you feel that if you could
somehow tap or reroute it, you could power a new kind of
city.

a small rain
of copper

❧

Yesterday I woke up and, I don't know, could be it was the sound of the birds, but I was buzzing there, you know. Bones felt restless. Like maybe they should be doing something. I started up pacing around. Trying to figure out what the hell was wrong with me. Well, after a while I think I put my finger on it. It's spring. Work. Work to be done. And at the same time I remembered the house is sold, garden with it—I don't have to do anything.

Well, I sat down on the bed and looked around the room. Wagon by the door, the one I built for the grandkids. Old bird feeder on the dresser beside Mary's reading glasses. She doesn't use them anymore. I keep them anyway. And all the family pictures. As well as the picture of the farm taken from an airplane. Aerial, they call it.

I sat there for a long time. I know I should have felt relieved. And I guess I did, a little.

☙

Mom calls. Grandpa's fallen again. Cracked his hip. Landed himself in hospital.

His life is peeling off him. In one swipe, two layers, at least: his apartment, his mobility. Astonishing how quickly he's lost the use of his legs. So the outer layers go. Closer and closer to the bone. We clear out his apartment. He'll never live alone again.

An incomplete list of items in my grandfather's apartment: A litre jar of local honey, half-full. The seagull ball-cap from PEI with fake bird-shit on it. An enamel jug and basin, mismatched. The old wooden coffee grinder. Two of every kind of screwdriver. The bird clock. Uncle Alf's bell collection. Two round tin canisters, one for sugar (labelled in two languages) and one for tea (labelled in three, his shaky hand all the way around). A bushel of apples, dried to fit in a shopping bag. The Lawren Harris print of the glacier. His harmonicas. Seven shaving soaps. Sandy, the canary. A chest freezer full of garden produce, some of it dating back twelve years. A spool of string, tall as a forearm and thick as a tree trunk when it ceases to be a sapling and becomes a tree.

For each item: Will he need this want this like this miss this in his room at the nursing home when he gets out of the hospital? (No one asks, will he ever see that room?) If no (he will not need this want this miss this), does somebody want to take this home? If yes (somebody wants it), and more than one person wants it, who should take it? Who has already taken what? Who isn't here who might want or deserve it? (There are criteria both spoken and unspoken.) If yes, and only one person wants it, fine. If no (nobody wants it), what do we do with it? Auctioneer? Salvation Army? Garbage? What is it worth?

No one asks will he ever see that room. He will not need this want this miss this. Somebody wants it. Nobody wants it. There are criteria both spoken and unspoken.

(What is it worth?)

The nurse comes in to give Grandpa a sponge bath, my cue to take my leave, head back to the city. He gives her a savvy wink and she smiles, says, "Now you behave yourself Mr. Friesen," wagging her finger as she pulls the curtain, gamely following the script. I wait a second at the door, listen in. His voice is shaky, but he's singing.

> Oh when I was young and in my prime
> I used to do it all the time.
> Now I'm old and getting grey
> I only do it once a...

I probably wouldn't let a man make innuendoes with me like that at the bar, but would I at the nursing home?

Whatever the case, right now I love her for allowing him the dignity of humour.

֍

"And who darns your socks?" the nurse asks Grandpa as she's putting them onto him.

"I do." His speech is agonizingly slow, but the nurse is patient. "Me, myself and I. Not the neatest job in the world. But it works by God."

She whistles and says, "You're a rare man Mr. Friesen, darning your own socks."

"That's," he pauses, taking a long while to swallow, "my mother."

"She taught you?"

"Oh yes. Punishment. Best punishment she ever invented."

༄

Good Friday is the day we agree on for clearing out Grandpa's apartment. He's still in the hospital, growing thinner and thinner, oxygen tubes in his nose, IV in his wrist, a string to call the nurses safety-pinned to his gown. He lies there tied, bird-boned and awkward.

We spend most of the day in separate rooms—Mom in the kitchen, Uncle Nick in the bedroom, me in the living room—cleaning, boxing, sorting. Every once in a while, one of us wanders to another room for company, then wanders back to our task. At one point, Uncle Nick strides into the living room, showing me an armful of shaving soaps.

"I distinctly remember throwing out at least a dozen shaving soaps when we sold the house and taking home a half-dozen more," he says. "How many shaving soaps does one man need?"

Mom hears us and comes in from the kitchen, bearing a massive spool of string.

"Okay," she says, "who wants this? If you take it, it's a commitment. We had one of these spools in the shed on the farm growing up, remember Nick? I still remember the day—I must have been thirteen or fourteen—when I went out to the shed to get some string for a package Mom was wrapping, and there it was, the last piece. I was stunned. Couldn't believe there was actually an end to it. It had always just been there."

No one else wants his knives so I take them all, wooden-handled, thin-edged, curved concave with years of sharpening—seven of them, fanning like feathers from cleaver down to paring knife. I also take his whetstone.

I've never sharpened knives before. Now there is this inheritance: the peeling away of a layer of his life, the laying on of a layer of mine. I'm sharpening my new knives daily. The sound of steel against stone draws me in. More and more I feel myself part of the cycle, the order of things—unchoosing, almost animal. Cutting is different now. I've always had cheap, dull knives; I've always cut with force. Now the introduction, the thin entrance of the blade. Smooth. Charming. I draw one of his knives through an onion with almost no resistance.

There's a superstition about the need to pay for the gift of a knife. Payment absolves the giver of any violence perpetrated with it. We haven't told him yet about the clearing out of his apartment, so Grandpa doesn't know that he's given me his knives.

I could drop seven pennies into the pocket of his coat that hangs in the hospital room locker.

I could stack seven pennies on the oxygen machine at his bedside.

Or, I could place them one after another in his palm and say it's in exchange for seven thoughts.

He's awake lately only for a minute at a time—half a sentence at most. Again and again I watch his eyes close, his fists release. If I were to pay for the gift of the knives, he'd drop each penny one by one. When I left there would be pennies scattered among his sheets. When the nurses stripped the bed, a small rain of copper.

seven thoughts for seven pennies for seven knives

it's about time that

        I'll be damned if

    can you hear the

            when I was a nurse I

lilacs are the only

         I used to love it when

   listen here—

❧

At Easter dinner, my cousin Max's girlfriend is talking about a quiz she found on the internet which can supposedly detect your gender by how you answer a series of questions. Questions like, *Would you rather have your bedroom painted blue or white? Would you rather work first and have fun later, or vice versa?* One question in particular makes me look up from my ham. *Would you rather be desperately lonely for the rest of your life or slowly bleed to death right now?* I don't catch which answer means you are a woman, but I do catch myself thinking with a deep unforeseen gladness which spreads in a wave from my torso to my fingertips, I'd rather be lonely. No question.

Getting up from the table to go pee, I bend to kiss James on the neck as I pass him, and my heart gives a clutch at how heartened and surprised he looks.

Clara and the triplets arrived late. She looks exhausted, says she's taken to not wearing her seatbelt. I realize I don't really believe in other people's suffering much of the time. The triplets keep eyeing me as if I have an absurd haircut. Maybe I do.

Every few minutes I remember that Grandpa is in the hospital, probably dying.

Watching Clara with her triplet toddlers—the moment by moment decisions, when to chastise, when to console, what to emphasize and command, what to discourage and ignore, what to laugh off—it strikes me how short a distance good intentions take us. I used to think I could coast on them all the way home, but I'm coming to see they only barely get you started. After that you need assorted things like humour, bloody-mindedness and luck.

Uncle Nick is teaching the kids "Ninety-nine Bottles of Beer on the Wall" as payback to Clara for her childhood. Also a song that goes,

> *This is the song that never ends*
> *Yes it goes on and on my friend*
> *Some people started singing it not knowing what it was*
> *And they'll continue singing it forever just because*
> *This is the. . .*

❧

In all my eighty-eight years, he says, *this is the fastest I've seen it.* Each word is separate, slow—thick-skinned bubbles launched through a heavier air. When they burst, heard, the room is washed by the hollowness they held. It's the first full sentence he's spoken in English in days.

Lately he's taken to speaking in Low German, his mother tongue. The nurses call it delirium, but sometimes, when we're alone, he translates. *Ich kann nicht verstehen.* I lean in close. Five minutes later, eyes closed: *I can't understand.* As I leave, his eyes still closed: *Adieu, Adieu, Adieu.* Three white handkerchiefs hung out one by one on the line.

Today I'm talking to him about spring, about the leaves coming out—how improbable the green, how quick, how if you're not careful you miss it. I'm just talking, not expecting a reply. He has a view of the treetops from his hospital window. Then, like an upper branch showing up in full leaf one morning on a tree you took for dead, he says, *In all my eighty-eight years, this is the fastest I've seen it.*

I asked Mom the other day if it's true that time goes faster as you get older. "Oh Lord yes," she said. "Faster and faster every year."

I think of those centrifugal force rides at the midway where you stick to the wall and your cheeks slide out of position and you can't lift your head or even move sometimes. Round and round so that, by the end, the most you can hope to focus on is not swallowing your tongue.

Grandpa in his hospital bed, not answering.

≈

You don't have to do much to speak volumes in your last days. He'd make a batch of muffins and a pot of coffee and invite a nursing home volunteer up to his apartment to share them, and it was a grand gesture, containing a lifetime. Each day, on his way to visit her in Extended Care, he walked around the atrium of the old age apartments bearing the cockatiel on his shoulder, and it was an act stunning in its generosity.

Terrible to say, in a way, but there's a glamour in decay. All the sugars rising to the surface. Even the making of wine is a kind of controlled decomposition.

The last days have an atmosphere in which everything stands out, backlit, finite. Photographers call it magic hour. As if death, closer now, closer every day, radiates a kind of pre-storm light.

And then that pre-storm light lasts for a spell after death—for the living. Basic things take on new definition, demand attention but resist naming. The world flares and rears under me these days in areas I always thought of as solid ground (or, more precisely, didn't think of at all). I slide off the slippery fact of things existing. I say to myself, you could spend your whole life saying to yourself, this could be the last time I ride a ferry, see a black and white movie, taste brandy, stand on tiptoe, roll out pie dough, write a letter, stamp it and drop it in the mailbox, see a fox up close.

I want to count each time in my life James brushes an eyelash from my cheek, want to tell each recurring dream— the one with the violin, the one with the teeth. Each grudge is a tightly sewn parcel safely storing a wound. Each brick was laid by a human hand: evidence.

That very soon Peter Friesen will never again have an itch he can't reach or the tang of vinegar on the sides of his tongue makes me feel each itch and tang as a responsibility.

There is a last time we each will swallow water.

୶

They've not told me, no not in so many words, but I know. It's not likely I'll be going home. That's fine and dandy, I want to tell them—it's not home anyway, that apartment. Sold the house when was it, last spring? And twenty years or more before that we sold the farm. And it was long before that when I last saw the land where I was born. Don't talk to me about home, I want to say. *Dad*, they say, *you sold the farm twenty years ago*. To rub my face in it. Then they tell me all about some other room they've set up for me in the nursing home, *a nice tree outside the window*, they keep saying. You're all goddamn fools I want to say. They're the ones who're confused. *We told you Dad*, they say, patient voices like a slap-dash whitewash job. *We have to be realistic*, they say. *You can't go back to the apartment. It's a beautiful room, and you'll be taken care of there.* I lose track of which story I'm supposed to be going along with. Pretending I have a home, pretending I'll walk again, pretending I care. Pretending we don't all know the only way I'm getting out of this place is in a box. They can't even draw blood anymore. Three different nurses tried yesterday. Sticking me again and again. Veins drying up like a creek in drought.

Oh they skirt around it so carefully that I know it better than if they just came right out with it. And I hear them when they're talking to each other and I've got my eyes closed because I can't manage to even lift my lids let alone say something in response to all their questions. Sometimes after I've sat up the whole morning and lifted the fork to my mouth so many times in a row I want to holler or throw something or even weep but I wouldn't have the energy, even if I had it in me to let myself go like that, and then the lunch tray arrives and after all that lifting I've barely even made a dent in breakfast, and I tell you I get to a place where the air itself is so heavy the smallest fraction of a nod feels as if I'm heaving myself up out of bed to stand at the window. Then one of them will show up like they think they're the second coming and say, *Look Dad, your lunch,* and I just want to close my eyes and be gone.

The funny part is how fast it happens when you can't bring yourself to make a sign you hear them, how fast they begin to assume you're not there. They think I'm asleep and I can't tell them there is a difference between this place and sleep.

I want to tell them there was a time when I threw a football, perfect spiral, over the barn. There was a time when I pitched a shovelful of soil over my shoulder to another place with less effort than it takes now to lift a tissue and receive the bit of gristle I've finally worked from the back of my mouth to my lips. There was a time when my legs held me upright all day long and on into the twilight and when I sat down to the evening meal those legs waited, buzzing and bent and ready for anything. I close my eyes and remind myself there was a time when I moved easily. Effortlessly. It's a kind of torture to think of it, but I tell you it's the only direction in my mind left to go that isn't closing up like my veins. I think of that easiness as a kind of country now. A place. One I'll never see again. But when I close my eyes sometimes I can get a glimpse of it. Even straining under the weight of a sack of grain or struggling with a plough had an ease about it and I wonder now whether it was the hope or the muscle that made it easy. Not that I can remember the feeling of it. Limbs closing up shop. No feeling. So it's just the picture in my head. Like a photograph of the Old Country. Same way that after Mother died I could look at a photograph of her till kingdom come, but it never gave me back what it was to sit across the kitchen table from her flesh and bones, never gave me back the feeling, you know. The inside of the feeling. The feeling that even if you knew exactly what she would do or say next, even if you knew her that well, as I knew Mother, well, she could still surprise you. Even if she didn't.

I lift my eyelids and it's like rolling away a stone heavier than myself. Just in time to see the nurse leaving the room, tucking her hair behind her ear without the slightest thought, as if she were a chosen one. As if she'd never die.

⁊

Last night I gave a woman the last bath of her life. Ginny.
Her legs have grown too weak to get in and out of the tub.
It's too dangerous to try to lift her. From now on she'll have to
be taken to the shower room down the hall. Ginny loved her
baths. *Oh well*, she sighed when I had her out and powdered
and pyjama'd and sitting on the side of her bed, frail as a girl.
She folded her hands and looked up at me, finding the shaky
footing of a smile, *You can't have everything.*

୬

The perennial order goes something
like this: crocus, tulip, lilac, lily
of the valley, iris,
poppy, peony, and he

slips into the earth somewhere
between the lily of the valley
and the iris. Late
May. An early spring.

A week later, the stripped stamens
of the irises, the poppies with their red
cups empty, each peony balled up
like a kid glove waiting for a
hand and I'm thinking, *how well*
the poppies know their part,
thinking, *how strange*
the colour red, thinking,
                    too late—over and over the fact
of it fills
the glove.

fancy meeting
you here

᷒

We force Grandma's stiff arms into the dress she wore on their fiftieth wedding anniversary, manoeuvre her into a wheelchair and then, because it's a nice day and easier than getting her into a car, we push her along the sidewalk, past their old house, to the funeral home. She blinks in the midday, late-May light. She blinks at the traffic lights. She blinks at the bed of irises I point out to her, and then she looks up at me and blinks again.

I smile. She smiles back.

When we get to the funeral home, we push her right up to the side of the coffin. Mom kneels beside her and explains, as if to a child, "It's Peter. Your Peter. Dad. He's died, Mom. We brought you so you could say goodbye."

And she blinks and blinks as if at a light too bright.

There isn't much crying; it seems time. After the funeral, we manoeuvre Grandma out of the wheelchair and into the car. The procession winds slowly from the funeral home through town toward the cemetery. The undertaker drives the lead car at the pace of a walk. We creep down the hill, ease onto Main Street. Cars stop. People stop. I'm dry-eyed until I realize they're stopping for us.

Then I cry, and honestly I couldn't tell you why I'm crying. Perhaps because people in small towns still know to stop when a funeral passes. Or because people in cities don't. Or for the life that begs this pause. Or maybe I'm crying for us all. For us all walking unaccountably dry-eyed over the earth.

＆

New Year's Day, 1932

As I said everything is going fast
and where a poor guy knows it first
is when he starts counting the few slippery greenbacks
which he has earned by pulling four horses
and the implement
and pulling cows teats of course.
About the hired girl Jean Wilson there is little to write
though I know plenty
about her. All I can say is Youth
will have its fling and she certainly had hers
and how. Poor kid in a way I feel sorry for her but
oh well who am I to take life serious I'm free
in a free country
so here goes—whoopee
for 1932!

ॐ

What does that mean Grandpa?

What? Eh?

That curse you always say. What does it mean?

Come again?

You know, *ay-ay-ay, matoushka ri-nanka,* or whatever it is.

Yessir and what about it?

What does it *mean?*

Damned if I could say now.

Oh come on. You must know what it means.

Of course I know what the goddamn thing means. It's just to try to switch it over and get it across to you what it means is a whole other kettle of fish goddammit.

Just give me a general idea then.

Alright, alrighty. If it means that much to you. Let's see. Close as I can come is something to do with your mother, a goat, and a bolt of lightning.

Your mother a goat and a bolt of lightning?

That's right. You do the math.

❧

things buried with us (2)

1

Lately James and I have been eating only soup and bread.
Funny what happens when the hunger
to be simple is whetted daily;
after a while it stops being dull.

2

He rowed before he knew me, and I love this
odd and unimportant detail (come to me
from that time like someone else's keepsake):

rowers face backwards so he'll
always have starboard and port reversed.

How my head is
hushed and my skin strokes
hot at the thought of his
unknown hands at
dawn on those oars.

3

When we fight we
go from room to
room, closing doors
behind us, then

opening them again
moments later.

4

I notice we put on our t-shirts differently:

I shake my arms into the
sleeves first then slip my
head through the
neck hole as quickly as
possible so as not to
miss a thing.

He lassoes the whole thing over his head and pulls it down.
Then he pushes his arms up through, as if climbing
out of a manhole.

5

Sometimes when I hug him around the neck he lifts
me just a little to his height,
my back crackles into alignment
and then he sets me down again,
taller.

~

There's a man who travels
the sidewalks of my neighbourhood
in a wheelchair pulled by huskies.
I see him often at intersections,
two dogs panting, waiting
for the light to change.
At the exact moment it turns
green they spring
forward so if you didn't know better
you'd be confused
(do they trigger the light,
or the light,
their movement?).

They pass the dishevelled man who stands
barefoot in undone sneakers no matter what
the weather, one leg of his track pants
lodged up around his shin,
the other, ragged
under his heel.
He stands at the same
intersection all day long,
conducting traffic,
urging the cars forward and back
in perfect unison with the traffic lights.

This, perhaps, is as likely as anything else to
turn out to be
what makes the world go around.

The man in the wheelchair calls *yee* and *haw*
for right and left,
speaking the same language
my grandfather spoke behind his plough horses
once upon a time.

As they glide away
you can almost hear
the earth turning in response,
the *shshsh* of sled runners over snow,

can almost bear
to call the city home.

Someone has tapped a maple tree
in the parkette down the street.
I think now I'll be able to sleep at night knowing
somewhere nearby there is an apartment,
windows fogged with steam—
                              shshshsh

—when it's all boiled down there will be just enough
to fill a teacup,
a bird's nest,
a bell.

One garbage day
my neighbour Connie
spotted an old leather couch on the curb
on her way to trade in her empties—
the springs in the couch were
shot, so she skinned it.

Connie is Ojibway,
makes dream catchers
with couch leather and seagull feathers
dyed eagle.

I'm standing at the intersection, waiting
for the streetcar. I see her pass
with her bundle buggy, waving.
I wave back, aware I'm only
human but hoping I have the human
touch. When you say the word
human, do you mean it
as excuse or incantation? Ask me

and I am torn
between the two,
again and again my head
turned by how we make
do   on the way
to trade in
our empties.

∾

Well, we got out of doing the dishes, didn't we Grandma?
Although you always said you liked doing dishes, right?

I know what place
I should be now   I think

It's okay Grandma, you're fine right here. Just relax. Okay?
We'll go back in when they call us for pie. Okay?

(pointing to the ploughed garden) like that

(silence)

I love watching the leaves fall.
You like fall, don't you Grandma?

(silence)

You're looking at the wind chimes.
Do you like the wind chimes Grandma?

if you call it right

Call it right?

I should name it

You should name it?

I should
but I don't think it wants to be named

(silence)

Fall's my favourite season.
Do you have a favourite season Grandma?
What's your favourite season?

I don't think
there's any pie left
for me

~

I need to leave now Grandpa. I have to catch my train so I can be back in the city by nightfall. Make sure the nurses are good to you. And don't let the doctors do anything to you that you don't want them to do.

oh   you took   the train   did you?

(*nodding*) It's a nice day—a good day for a train ride. I like to choose a seat by the window and read a book.

and look up   out the   window   now and then?

Yes.

you better go then   the train won't

(*silence*)

Wait for me?

yes

Acknowledgements

The opening quotation from Jan Zwicky is from *Songs for Relinquishing the Earth*, Brick Books, 1998, page 13, used by her kind permission.

The passages on pages 39, 57 and 76 are from *Alzheimer: A Canadian Family Resource Guide* by Lori Kociol and Myra Schiff, McGraw Hill, 1989, pages 10 to 12. Used by permission of the authors.

The entries on page 89 are from *Mind Your Manners: A Complete Dictionary of Etiquette for Canadians*, by Claire Wallace, edited by Joy Brown, Harlequin Books, 1953.

Passages on pages 7, 8, 18, 19 and 240 are inspired by (and in some cases are modified quotations from) the diaries of Peter and Mary Papky.

The line referenced on page 64 is from *Once in Europa* by John Berger.

Thank you to the Ontario Arts Council and the Toronto Arts Council for financial support during the writing of this book. Thanks also to the Banff Centre for the Arts.

Parts of this book appeared (sometimes in slightly different form) in the *Malahat Review*, *Geist* and *Breathing Fire 2: Canada's New Poets*; my thanks to the editors of these publications.

Many people read and supported versions of this book (and of me) along the way. Thanks in particular to Kelly Aitken, Michelle Cameron, Kirsten Corson, Degan Davis, Scott

McLoughlin-Marratto, Don McKay, Jeremy Munce, Liz Philips, Alison Pick, Johanne Pulker, Joyce Redford (for her example of faithfulness), Jo Roberts, Doug Raisbeck, David Seymour, Sue Sinclair, Suzannah Smith, Alana Wilcox, the generous souls of Brick Books (Stan Dragland, Marnie Parsons and others) and the good people I wrote with in writing groups over the years. And thank you to Silas White and Kathy Sinclair at Nightwood Editions for, among other wonders, their trust in me.

I'd also like to thank all of the characters who appear in this book: friends, family, passing acquaintances and strangers, naked, in costume, in disguise, in the wings. Sometimes main characters show up as extras, walk-ons as stars. In all cases, the portraits are necessarily partial, because of our boundlessness and in service to the whole. My gratitude for all of you. As my grandmother used to say when she was losing her mind and needed a phrase that would fit any occasion, it takes all kinds.

Finally, this book is for my father, Greg Munce (1946-2002). Though he does not appear directly in these pages, he's behind every one.

About the Author

Alayna Munce has been published in various Canadian literary journals and in *Breathing Fire 2: Canada's New Poets* (Nightwood). She is a past winner of the CBC Literary Awards and a three-time winner of *Grain* magazine's Short Grain Contest.

Alayna Munce grew up in Huntsville, Ontario, and now lives in Toronto.